My Mute
Girlfriend

My Mute Girlfriend

HIMANSHU RAI

Srishti
PUBLISHERS & DISTRIBUTORS

SRISHTI PUBLISHERS & DISTRIBUTORS
Registered Office: N-16, C.R. Park
New Delhi – 110 019
Corporate Office: 212A, Peacock Lane
Shahpur Jat, New Delhi – 110 049
editorial@srishtipublishers.com

First published by
Srishti Publishers & Distributors in 2018

10 9 8 7 6 5 4 3 2 1

Dedicated to
Every couple that could not complete
their love story...

Acknowledgements

No words can thank the man for what I am today: My father, Late Shri Prafulla Kumar Rai.

Special thanks to my dear wife Sona and son Rhythm. Sharing our life and love on this journey together is a blessing beyond words.

Thanks to my mom, Meera Rai, for motivating me to pursue my dreams and never letting things go.

Thanks to Srishti Publishers, Mr J.K. Bose, Arup Bose for believing in my story and helping giving it shape. No book is complete without perfect editing, and I am thankful to Stuti for editing my script and for her valuable suggestions.

Thanks to my friends from Guru Ramdas Khalsa Engineering College, for being with me for my life. Special thanks to Anurag Thakur, Vineet Sinha and KK Pradeesh for allowing me to use them as an essential characters in my story.

Thanks a lot to my school, St. Joseph Convent for teaching me values in life.

Thanks to my friends, family and relatives for supporting my work and motivating me.

Year – 2003

My name is Rohan Verma, and that day, I felt on top of the world. The wind blew at a hundred and twenty kilometres per hour, trying to drag me away. It made it difficult for me to keep my eyes open as I was mesmerized by the beauty of nature, standing atop the hundred metre high mobile tower. From where I stood, everything looked tiny, almost as if I could fit it all in my pocket.

Khatuli, a small town near Meerut, could be seen in its entirety from the height. It was amazing to observe the mountains covered in the lush, beautiful green of the vegetation to my north. I leaned down a little with the support of the railing to check how my white Indica looked from above – like a toy car.

It was late evening, and the sun was turning red, all set to melt into the horizon. The birds had started to return to their nests, and sometimes I felt like they were wondering what a human was doing at a height only they soared. I turned back to the other side to check out Khatuli's famous highway restaurant, 'The Cheetal Grand', where I would be heading down for some tasty pakoras and chai.

The topmost mast of the tower looks narrow from the ground level, but the platform alone is big enough to fit a car. Enjoying the cool September breeze, I laid down on the platform and, using my hand as a pillow, admired the clear blue sky.

The place was quiet until I heard the *azaan* from a nearby mosque. It was pleasant to listen to the call to worship god. I closed my eyes to connect to the surrounding beauty. As I did, the song of the wind echoed in my ear, and I replied with one of my own:

"Main zindagi ka saath nibhata chala gaya... har fikra ko dhuein mein udata chala gaya.."

The song had me thinking this could be a perfect place to have a cigarette in peace. I pulled out a packet of Gold Flake carefully. I pulled out a cigarette and placed it between my lips as I dug into my pocket for a matchstick.

The wind blew wilder as if challenging me to light the cigarette. I loved challenges. I failed to light the first matchstick, but I wouldn't let that bring me down. So I said to the wind, "Oh! Trying to challenge me? I've been smoking for five years now, seen many like you."

I brought the cigarette between my lips closer to the matchbox and tried to light if faster than the wind could snuff out the flame, and, with the first puff of smoke, I declared my victory. I stood there, holding the railing and taking puffs in peace.

I leaned down again to check my vendor who was installing a microwave antenna about fifty metres down.

"Is it installed or do you need more time?" I shouted looking at the man hanging from the tower with security belts.

"Sir, just a bit longer. I'm almost finished," he replied with a shout.

A year back, I too was working with a small vendor company; working in severe and adverse conditions. Working in tough conditions was still manageable, but being an engineer and working as labour is quite embarrassing. That was the reason I was thankful to god for ending my struggle by helping me in joining Hutch mobile operator posted in Meerut.

We would soon launch mobile operations of Hutch in Uttar Pradesh and I was assigned the job to visit the mobile tower sites to see that all installation jobs were running as per schedule.

Back then, mobile operations were still not spread widely in India. Those were the years of the revolution in mobile handset penetration. Few people at the time used to carry mobiles and they were the privileged. I was just an engineer, but thankfully my company had given me a Nokia 3315 which I used to flash to impress women.

I finished my cigarette and looked up at the sun which had disappeared by then, giving way to a dark sky. The first star shone in the sky, and I remembered a line: *"Pehla dekhe paapi..."*

It was one game we used to play as kids. The first four visible stars in the sky decided our fates.

I remembered lines of the game and felt nostalgic: *"Pehla dekhe paapi, dusra dekhe raja, teesra dekhe shaitaan aur choutha dekhe pura sansaar..."*

It was time for me to get down before it got even darker. After pandiculating, I moved down the metal stairs coiling around the tower.

In my pocket, my mobile beeped and buzzed. I stopped to pull it out to check it, thinking it must be one of my vendor teams. I held on tight to the railing of the stairway, bringing the phone close to my face to read the message.

Can we talk? Vaidehi

My eyes stopped blinking, my heart froze, and it felt like the blood had stopped flowing in my veins as I read the message. A message from someone about whom, even after five whole years, I still thought every single day.

I banged my head on the railing to check if I was alive.

"Yes, it's true! She has sent me a message..."

I smiled as I moved back down, trying to put the mobile back into my pocket. But—

"Oh shit!"

The mobile fell in a straight line downwards. I rushed to chase after it, shouting to my vendors on the ground, "Hey guys, my mobile fell down, please catch it!"

I took long steps, running with no fear of tripping and falling on my face when there were hardly ten steps left.

As it fell, it banged against the tower rods, bounced on the roof of the equipment room below and plopped straight into a swamp.

I rushed towards the swamp while my vendors looked on from the sidelines.

"Sir, it sank on that side, near that big buffalo."

I stopped to think for a second, putting my hands on my hip and then went into the swamp.

"Sir, don't do this. That mobile is gone, you can just get another one from the office!"

But they didn't understand just how important it was to me right then. It had a message from Vaidehi after all. I rolled my pant legs up and glided into the swamp.

I looked for the device, searching desperately under the buffalo with my face uncomfortably close to it. But no matter what, I couldn't just leave the phone with Vaidehi' s message in the mud.

I kept on searching until my hands grasped something. It was my Nokia 3315. I pulled it out excitedly, wondering whether it would still work covered in mud and buffalo shit, with a broken screen and no life left in it. And yet, I was still happy to have it back. I pressed on the buttons repeatedly, desperately.

My vendor boy, who was looking at me strangely, put out his hand to pull me out from the swamp; maintaining his distance to protect his clothes.

"Sir, it's gone now, it won't work," he told me as if I didn't already know.

"It matters a lot even if it doesn't work," I replied with a small smile.

He brought over a bucket of water and a mug. With them, I washed my mobile and myself.

I was upset. I didn't have Vaidehi's number, so I couldn't call her from my vendor's mobile either. Maybe she was waiting for my call and would now think I was still not interested in talking to her.

I sat down on the stairs to the equipment room next to the base of the tower. It was already dark by then and the vendor had packed up.

"Team, after pack up you may take rest for the day and then complete the next site in Roorkee tomorrow. I'll be leaving for Dehradun now and will call you once I collect my new handset tomorrow. You can continue with your work now," I instructed since I would be out of contact for a day.

I put my laptop bag on my shoulders and grabbed my shoes in one hand and asked my driver to bring the cab over so we could leave for Dehradun.

I boarded my cab, and we started towards the highway. As Khatuli was a very small town, we crossed it in about ten minutes. I was both happy and confused as I wondered why she had messaged me after five long years.

"I hope that wasn't a prank from one of my old college friends. I don't have her number, after all. Maybe one of my friends was trying to prank me by sending a message using her name. But then, what if it was her?" I'd been mulling over all these possibilities as the car entered the Dehradun Highway.

"Rajesh, we'll stay in Dehradun tonight, so let's try to reach there on time." I informed my driver as I lit another cigarette.

"You sure smoke a lot, sir," he remarked.

I smiled, looking out of the open car window.

"Yes well, someone once showed me it didn't matter to her whether I lived or died. So, I've been trying to kill myself since then." Hearing this, he burst out laughing.

Rajesh had been my driver for the past year and he was more like a friend by then. He's a passionate guy and wants to learn a lot in his life.

Moving past trees, small huts with yellow bulbs and roadside vendors, always excited me during a drive. But today, my mind was elsewhere. Her thoughts had overtaken my body, drowning it in her memories.

1998
Sagar, a small city in Madhya Pradesh

It was 2 a.m. and I was sitting at my study table with my chemistry book open in front of me, with the night lamp focused on the book, its light spreading to the corners of the room. Having completed my schooling the previous year, I had taken a drop year to prepare for engineering entrance exams. There was a heavy silence in the room, the only sound being the noises of insects coming from outside my window.

Rotating the pencil in my fingers, I looked at the framed picture placed on my desk. It was a picture from school, back when I was the school Captain. Beside me stood the Vice-Captain Navya, who had been in class 11th. I was holding the school emblem for a practice where the captain from class 12th and the vice-captain from class 11th held up the school's emblem. It was a proud moment for me. But the picture wasn't just that of a proud moment; it was also a picture of Navya, whom I admired a lot through my last year of school. Or perhaps I should say I loved her a lot during my school days.

She was my first love or crush and it had been my dream to be with her forever. During my final year, I used to go to school daily, even when my friends stopped coming to school to prepare for the boards and entrance exams, just to meet her.

She always met me with a smile on her face and that was what brought me to school every day. That reminds me; I managed getting a second division in the twelfth because I concentrated more on the dimple on her left cheek than I did on my studies.

"Oh god help me; I want to study now and clear my engineering entrance exams." If I became an engineer, I could propose to her and she wouldn't say no, I was sure of that.

After I had completed my twelfth, I took a year off to prepare myself for the engineering exams. I never proposed to her as I thought I was too young to propose to someone. I decided, after seeing my second division results, to concentrate on my engineering entrance and contact her once I made it into a good engineering college.

I moved my eyes back to my chemistry book and tried to understand the characteristics of Crystalline Solids and Amorphous Solids. I tried to give my full attention to chemistry and started repeating the definitions. I read them twice from the book, then closed it and started repeating them, and yet again my eyes went to the photo on my desk.

I stood up and moved to my cupboard behind me. I opened the cupboard and pulled out a silver diary with a red rose printed on its cover. This was my poem diary. I used to write poems when I was eleven or twelve years old, but the passion grew after

I met her. I felt I should write one more for her so I could get her out of my mind and concentrate on my studies.

I took my diary and pen from my desk and went to my bed. My room was beautiful, and all set for studying. Every corner of the walls looked covered with formulas, periodic tables, important questions, etc. It was only her picture that gave me the strength to study and study harder. When I was in school, I used to talk to her on the landline. But I hadn't called her in the past six months. I still believed she would be waiting for me to call, but I had decided that I would only call her once I got into an engineering college. It was a time when I needed to behave like a strong, committed man. But somewhere in my heart, I was always scared. What if she found someone better than me in the meantime?

Whatever, I was sure she loved me too and would wait for me. I wrote my poem and by the time I was done, I was sleepy. That day again, her dimples had won over chemistry.

I feel that there are chemistries that exist in this world, other than the bulky chemistry I study in my books. Like the chemistry of first love, the chemistry of eyes and the chemistry of smiles. I needed to study hard to make my chemical experiment a success, but I was asleep by then.

Next morning, I woke up at 6 as I had my Physics tuition classes at 7.30 a.m. I got ready and hurried to my class. My mom was worried about me as I skipped breakfast that day in my hurry to get to class. My elder sister Surbhi, however, was suspicious of me.

Surbhi was five years older than me. Navya was the cousin of her close friend. She used to get information about what I did in school from her friend. Since then she had been wanting to prove to my mother that the photo on my desk was kept, not out of pride of being Captain, but because Navya was in it.

But whenever she tried to prove this, I made an innocent face at my mom and said she was just jealous of me because she could never be captain herself. We might fight each other, but I knew once I completed engineering, she was the only person who would help me, through her best friend, to marry Navya. And I was working hard towards my goal.

I attended the two-hour long class and came back home at 10 a.m. I asked my mother to give me something to eat as I was starving. My sister sat next to me, looking like she'd just won a gold medal in the Olympics for India.

"Are you not studying at night Rohan?" Mom asked me with a tense look.

I looked at her innocently. I knew where the medal hung now.

"What happened, Mummy?" I replied to her.

My sister slid my poem diary towards me on the table. I hadn't noticed it was there till then.

"What happened?" I asked again.

"You're not concentrating on your studies again and just focusing on the photo girl," Mom told me sternly, continuing, "She ruined your twelfth result, now you will ruin your entrance results. Your father is working so hard every day, but you are just not bothered. We told you, first begin a career and then we'll let you marry whoever you want!"

"Mom, it's not for her, I love writing poems and I got ideas after listening to Jagjit Singh ghazals last night," I replied innocently. "I can assure you, I was studying till 2 a.m. See my marks in today's tuition test; I scored nineteen out of twenty!"

After looking at my marks, Mom cooled down and now the referee would take the medal that my sister had just won a few minutes back.

"And you, Surbhi! Why are you always after him? You should concentrate on your own exams, I'm sure he's working very hard," Mom scolded my sister.

Now I smiled as if the medal had been transferred to me as my sister had been caught doping.

Surbhi Di was looking at me angrily and I stared right back.

Those days, my only job was to eat and study. I studied for fifteen hours, ate for three hours and slept for six. I had put on fifteen kilograms in the last six months, and I was tired of studying all the time. Everyone in my family and all my relatives were waiting for me to clear my entrance exams. Some of them already considered me an engineer. A few days back, my cousin's bike wouldn't start, and my aunt came expecting me to repair it because I was studying to be an engineer!

My life revolved around physics, chemistry, maths and dimples. But the dimples which had been the most important had fallen to a status of low priority by then.

My exams were nearing, and I needed to really focus. I was busy revising everything and attending mock tests every day to know where I stood with my preparation. I forgot the dimples for the next few months and removed her photo from my desk and kept it in my diary instead.

I talked to her through the picture and told her, "Just for a few days dear, this is just because I want to come to you fast."

One day, when I stood discussing a few physics problems with my friends after tuition class, my eyes wandered over to a restaurant on the other side of the road. Through the glass door, I could see Surbhi Di sitting and eating something. I thought she must've been hanging out with her friends after college and continued the discussion with my own friends.

But my eyes still hovered her way and after some time she came out with a boy. She sat on the backseat of his bike and they took off.

Where was her scooty? Who was that boy?

I was thrilled to have witnessed this; it was like I had won my very own medal. But I thought I could use this extra benefit for myself. Perhaps it could come of use in future battles.

I returned home that afternoon to find that she wasn't home from college. I went to study in my room and then to another class. When I returned at night, I saw her helping mom with work. I decided not to talk to her about it, not yet.

After dinner, Surbhi Di also came up to my room to study. I was struggling with a numerical. She sat on the corner of the bed with a pillow behind her and her book in hand while I sat on my study table.

"Who were you with at the restaurant?" I asked her while I kept on reading my book.

She was shocked, but tried to be cool.

"Who? What are you talking about?"

Now I turned towards her with my hand on the back of my chair. "I saw you today with a boy in Sadar Market and then you left with him on his bike."

She now knew that she was caught and that the medal was in my hands. She was ready to surrender. She closed her book, made a face and came closer to me on the bed.

"Bhai, please Mummy ko nahi kehna," she said, smiling at me.

"What should I not tell her?" I tried to be a little childish.

She continued, "He is my boyfriend and studies with me in my class. I'll take you to meet him. He is very nice, but please don't tell Mummy for now. I will tell her when the time comes."

I looked at her and realized that she was in the same boat as me, waiting for the right time. Like I was waiting for the right time to speak to Navya and then my parents. And I knew she was the only one who could take me back to Navya after the next five years when I complete my engineering. I couldn't take *panga* with her at any cost; it was a matter of the dimples after all.

But I tried to show some attitude, "Don't worry, I won't tell her, but you will also have to help me when I need you."

She smiled and hugged me.

"I love you, bhai!"

Old people say that the perfect love can bring any change in a person and their life. See, that day I had a superb chance to take the gold medal from her, but my love complications stopped me. And that day, I learned that love teaches you politics as well.

I stood up and took my poem diary from the cupboard.

"What are you doing?" she asked me.

I gave her a confident look.

"I am writing a poem and you will say nothing to Mummy now," I replied.

She smiled. "Show me! I like to read them. Oh and there is one more thing I want to tell you."

"What?" I asked.

"Do you know how I came to know that you have written poems?" she told me

"How?" I asked again.

"I used to copy your love poems for my boyfriend Anuj," she mumbled.

Oh my god! So was I such a big poet. My poems were being circulated!

I smiled at her and told her she could use them anytime.

It was mid-May and my entrance exams were over. I felt like a free bird. I was determined to drop the weight that I had gained. I was getting ready for a funky college life.

One day, I got up at 5 a.m. to jog to my friend Vikram's house. He was my childhood friend. Mornings were still pleasant during the hot summer. I could see him from a distance – stretching down to touch his feet. Vikram had also taken a year off, and we both studied and went to the coaching classes together. As he saw me approaching, he jogged to join me, and we both started towards the main road.

"Bhai, Rohan, bahut phat rahi hai," he said to me while jogging.

I kept running as this was a patent dialogue of Vikram's. His mornings began with the refrain.

"What happened now?" I asked.

I pulled out my towel to soak the sweat on my face, while he replied, "Last night, Renu Didi called and pointed out to Papa that getting in IIT is difficult now as there is so much competition. According to her, my preparation was not up to that level." His sister Renu was in IIT Delhi.

"So what are you tensed about? You know you did well in the IIT entrance," I replied.

He halted, with his hands on his waist, taking deep breaths.

"What happened, tired?" I asked looking back at him. He looked towards the road, thinking. I moved towards him and asked.

"*Kya hua be?* Why so worried?"

"I did not appear for the IIT entrance, Rohan," he replied slowly. My eyes opened wide in shock.

I was always sure I was not an IIT type boy, so I did not apply, but Vikram, the brother of an IITian was always expected to be the next IIT candidate from our coaching classes.

Shocked and astonished, I said, "What? Bastard, do uncle and aunty know this?"

"If they had known, *toh meri phat ti kya?*"

"You're giving me shock after shock, Vikram. What are you saying?"

"Yes, that's right. I know I had not prepared enough for IIT, so on the day of the entrance, I went to watch *Kuch Kuch Hota Hai,*" he replied with a tense face.

"And then?" I asked him.

"Nothing, the movie was fantastic" he replied like a fool.

"I am asking about the entrance exam?"

"I told everyone at home that my exam didn't go well," he replied.

I thought for a while and then smiled at him. "When the result is declared, only the cleared roll numbers will be on the list, so chill and smile dear."

"Are you sure Rohan?" he asked, still tensed.

"*Pakka*, don't worry." Convincing him, I pulled at his hands and asked him to jog. He relaxed and smiled.

We reached to a point from where one road goes towards our school and the other takes a U-turn back towards his house. Vikram stopped at that point.

"The time has come to meet Navya, Rohan."

I kicked a stone with my left foot. "Not yet, my friend. I have not got into an engineering college yet."

"Don't miss a chance that is already waiting for you," he replied like a love guru.

"I believe that if she is a missed chance, then she is not meant for me," I replied.

But today, he was not listening to me; he was not ready to turn around. He forced me to jog to the school. I too was interested in getting a glance of her so I agreed with him and we jogged on.

We felt nostalgic. The place where you had spent thirteen years of your life, with friends, teachers and girls on whom you had your first crush, can never fade from your memory.

We stopped at the local canteen outside our school and asked for two cups of tea; our eyes on the school girls moving out from the school bus at the main gate.

The canteen shop owner gave us our tea, and we waited for Navya's school bus to arrive. It would be almost a year since I saw her last. "*Aaj propose hi kar de bhai,*" Vikram poked me.

But I was Mr Cool or a bloody fool who believed that I must not propose and wait till I finish engineering college. We took sips of tea while the buses kept on coming to drop the students off.

I never understood why our minds always dictate our hearts. And the heart, which is one of the most confused parts of the human body, keeps listening to the mind.

And then our wait was over as the mini bus in which Navya used to come to school arrived at the gate. Vikram gripped my shoulders, I put my cup of tea down, unblinking. My heartbeats could be heard by Vikram too, my legs were shaking, and my throat went dry.

One by one, students moved out from the bus, but we could not see her. I lost hope, thinking that maybe she was absent.

"Bhai, I think she is absent," Vikram spoke, while my eyes were still on the bus door, not losing hope. And then two fair hands came out from the door, holding the support rod of the bus gate, and then the left leg was put out. I saw her face, with blunt cut hair style and a big smile, chatting with her friend with her dimples out in all their glory.

Her eyes were blazing with joy, and it looked like she was the only one on earth without any tension in life. She looked amazing in the school uniform. She stepped out and then jumped to check someone peeping into the bus window. She then walked inside to the school gate with her friend. She looked at me, maybe expecting me to walk up to her, but I restrained myself, and she continued, keeping her eyes on me.

"I am telling you to propose or else let me do it," Vikram poked me again

"*Pagal hai kya,* she looks beautiful man. Thanks for bringing me here. I feel like I can live a hundred years without food and water now," I replied to Vikram.

I had no more energy to jog. I asked Vikram to walk back. As I saw her, every moment spent with her in the last one year of school, flashed before me. Her smile, her eyes, her voice. It seemed like it had only been a day since I was with her – smiling, teasing and enjoying some of life's best moments.

But someone had said that time gone is a moment missed and now only memories were left to be cherished.

I skipped going to the gym that day and reached home with her face in my eyes. I was smiling, loving that morning, hearing everyone but listening to no one. I went straight to my room and pulled out my dairy which had her picture hidden inside.

I pulled it out, looked at it with a smile on my face, caressed it with my hands and spoke to my heart, "*I miss you.*"

I was at a stage of my life when everything looked beautiful, everything looked fresh and everything looked young. I wanted to smile till the end of the day; I wanted to laugh till I went to sleep. I was spending a lot of time in the bathroom, just admiring my biceps and abs; practicing to propose in front of the mirror was my favourite pastime those days.

Laying buried in my bed, I dreamed during the day that I was in engineering college and during my vacations, I was running to my school in the bright sunlight with a red rose in my hand to where she was waiting to meet me, behind the old-school building. I hugged her and kissed her dimples and she smiled with love in her eyes. I said to her softly, coming close to her ears, "*I missed you.*"

I pulled myself out of my bed and looked at the watch which showed 3 p.m. I stood up and went to the kitchen, had a glass of water and then moved to check if Mom and Papa were awake. I peeped through the door and found them asleep. Surbhi Di was not at home; maybe she was with Anuj in college.

After seeing Navya, I was dying to hear her voice. I went to the drawing room where the land phone was. It was a hot summer afternoon, and I was wearing a white t-shirt and boxers to keep my body cool. I switched on the cooler placed in that room, to avoid any sound reaching my parents.

I made myself comfortable on the sofa and picked up the pale yellow BSNL phone and put it on my lap. Sweat flowed down my forehead as I dialled her number. It rang once, twice and then continued till she picked up from the other end and said "Hello... hello... who's there?"

I was silently, listening to her voice. It sank deep in my heart, making me restless. I could not hear even the sound of the Nagpur cooler, which was running like a helicopter in my room. I thought to reply and say "I miss you" but something kept holding me back.

She continued, "Whom do you want to talk to? Hello... please speak." But I kept holding back until she disconnected the call.

I placed the receiver back and smiled with my eyes closed, her face in front of my eyes. I stood up and went back to my room and again buried myself in my bed with her thoughts and memories. I tried closing my eyes to sleep, but every single time, I found myself awake, indulging in her memories and struggling between the past and the future.

God help me. When I wanted to stay awake, she made me sleep; now when I want to sleep, she is keeping me up. Is it because I miss her?

It was six in the morning on Sunday when my landline rang. My father picked up the phone to enquire who was calling that early in the morning.

"Oh, let me wake him up. And congrats to you!" he said and rushed towards my room. I could hear all this and was trying to figure out what was going on when Papa knocked on my door.

"Beta, get up, your pre-engineering test results are out in the local newspaper! Come fast with your roll number to the dining room. I am getting the paper."

My eyes opened wide in shock. There seemed to be no blood left in my veins and my ears buzzed, so I couldn't hear anything else. My heart was beating as fast as a train; I could feel the strain on my head. I jumped from my bed and pulled out my enrollment letter, which had my roll number on it.

I rushed to the dining hall and saw Papa wearing his specs and opening the newspaper, with my mother on his side and my sister behind him, holding a cup of tea. After seeing the faces of my parents, I understood what it meant to be parents; they looked more tense than me. My mother was praying, which was apparent from her face.

The cooker whistle broke me out of my thoughts and I ran towards them. I took the seat next to my father, and he passed the newspaper towards me. I checked the first three alphanumeric characters in the list, with my finger moving at the speed of light. I could not find my roll number in the first sheet.

"You are not in the top hundred, I think," Papa said.

I never understood why people wanted to be top rankers, because for me, whether I am in the top ten or last ten, I will still be an engineer, and that's all that matters.

I was sweating, and my head felt like it would burst, and my ears went red hot with each sheet I was turning.

Did I qualify or not? Do I need to repeat the entrance? Will my friends become my seniors? How will I convince Navya?

These questions where taking a hold of my mind, with each single line I crossed.

"I think you have not qualified," Surbhi Di interrupted.

I tried to ignore her, praying in my head. "*Oh God help me! Please let my name be there on the list!*"

And then my finger stopped. I found the first three letters of my roll number.

"Is it yours?" Papa asked in curiosity.

I kept checking the other digits to confirm if it's my roll number or not.

Yes, it looks like it is mine but let me recheck, I thought again.

"I got selected Papa. Mummy I got selected!" I yelled and touched their feet.

Mom kissed me on my forehead and thanked god. I hugged Surbhi Di.

Papa was extra happy on that day, but a little worried as my rank was three thousand thirty-four.

"Will you get any good college with this rank?"

I was worried as well, but tried to calm him. "Haan Papa, we will check during counseling. There are many new colleges coming up in Madhya Pradesh now," I continued, putting more sweets into my mouth which my mother gave me. "I'll meet some of my school seniors and will find out which are the good ones."

I brushed my teeth, took my sister's scooty and rushed to Vikram's house. I rang his doorbell and as uncle opened the door, I noticed a deep silence – no phone ringing, no sweets, no cousins, no chit chat. I doubted that he had qualified.

I took a seat on the wooden sofa which looked antique. I always used to tease Vikram about it. Vikram's father took the seat in front of me. He looked very dangerous; I was always scared of him. Whenever I saw him, I was reminded of Gabbar Singh from *Sholay*.

Wearing his white kurta pyjama, he looked at me with stern eyes. Above him hung a family photograph of Vikram's family in which uncle was standing in the centre and aunty, Vikram and his sister were standing next to him in attention position. It looked like they had been punished.

He asked me something with his eyes, which I could not understand and looked towards the door from where I was expecting Vikram to come out.

He then asked me in a booming voice, "What rank have you scored?" It sounded to me like the famous dialogue from *Sholay* – '*Kitne aadmi the?*'

"Three thousand and thirty-four," I replied in fear.

He showed no reaction. I tried to clear my ears to hear the word congrats, but could only hear the sound of the fan rotating.

"Vikram ranked seven hundred twenty. What will he get now? No good college, nor any good branch. I asked him to wait for JEEE results. I think he will do better in that," he said as I wondered if it was a taunt on my rank or whether he was really concerned about Vikram's rank. I felt that he had ranked well and he could go to whichever college he chose to. Because the JEEE results would never be out in his case.

Before I could have replied, Vikram came out of his room.

"Congrats man, you scored well," I stood up and hugged him.

"Thanks Rohan, but I'm not happy with my score. I must wait for the JEEE results. I am sure I will crack the IIT," Vikram replied looking at his father, while I could feel him pleading to not tell his father that he hadn't appeared in the IIT entrance exam.

Friends are the world's biggest saviors, especially in front of parents and this saying was proven on that day.

We went to our coaching institute to meet our other friends. On our way, I asked him, "Do you think I could get a college and branch of my choice?"

"Don't worry dear, if they have given you a rank, they would have reserved one college and branch for you," he replied coolly.

I smiled as we reached the coaching institute. I was depressed at seeing my friends with ranks within hundred and talking about some of the most prestigious colleges and branches.

But I was never good at studies, so even getting a rank at all was like winning a whole world for me. I believed god had something great for me in his kitty and would show it when the time came.

Along with Papa and Mummy, I reached Vyapam office in Bhopal at nine in the morning for my counselling on a day in the first week of June. As we reached its entrance gate, I was amazed to see so many students along with their parents, waiting outside in the heat for their turn to come.

I felt happy to see so many students like me, so I was not alone with a rank above three thousand. Papa and Mummy got comfortable positions under one tree and asked me to check when our turn was going to come.

I went to the main gate, which was closed with a shutter and a peon stood there to ensure no breach took place. I looked around and saw a blackboard on which was written,

'Entry from roll number 1200 to 1250'.

I understood, they were taking fifty candidates at a time for the counselling and my number would only come after a long wait.

I returned to inform Papa and saw he was talking to someone while looking at a brochure. As I reached him, he spoke to that person, proudly saying, "He is Rohan, and has got a rank in PET. You can tell him about your college."

"Hello Rohan, how are you? I am from St. Joseph College of Engineering and Technology Bhilai," he informed me, extending a brochure towards me. I took it and started looking at the lavish college building and green surroundings on the front page. While my eyes were on it, he continued, "This is the second year of our college and would like to tell you, we are among the best in technology in Bhilai."

I nodded at his words. Vikram had joined the Institute of Engineering and Technology, DAVV and I was eager to join another college in Indore, if not the same college. But I had to keep my options open.

He continued, "Bhilai is famous for industries, and engineers passing out from Bhilai would be first preference for them. We have excellent facilities and faculty…"

I kept on listening as he went on. Only one thing bothered me and that was that it was a missionary college and after fourteen years in a missionary school, I was reluctant to get into another one.

He moved on, but left a wonderful impression on my father.

"This is the best college for you. Been studying in St. Joseph School since the beginning, you will be comfortable there," Papa told me with confidence. He decided this college as the final one for me. My parents were so sure about this, that they started planning my stay with distant relatives in Bhilai.

But I was still confused and wanted to check out more options. I moved to other stalls to check if I could find something better and struggled to hear every single conversation happening for college selection discussions. It looked like colleges were on sale and we were moving in the market to find the best product to generate the best technical product in future. The morning turned to afternoon with the same discussions and more brochures in our hands. Mom pulled out the tiffin in which she had brought *parathas* and *sabji* as she knew that it would take time. We used the brochures as plates to have our lunch, and this was the best lunch we had after many days of tension. I was more relaxed now, seeing so many brochures in my hand, which confirmed that there were still many colleges waiting to make me an engineer. My mom was happy; now she could proudly say to her family that her son was an engineer. She served me an extra paratha in this happiness.

After lunch, I stood up and went to the entrance gate to check the blackboard. My turn was next! I ran towards Papa and asked him to hurry to the main entrance.

We walked to the gate and stood there, observing eager representatives from various colleges. The representative from St. Joseph Bhilai College smiled and showed me his hand from far to gesture to me that I must relax, as he had a seat already booked for me.

I too smiled and assured him that I would join his college. I was still not sure which college I would choose, but if I would get nothing good, I would opt for the Bhilai college.

The gate opened and we went inside. I saw a big balcony with multiple rooms. And more representatives selling their colleges. Colleges which got a room inside were better and older colleges, I suppose. We moved around to check out more options, creating more confusion.

"Which branch you are planning to take up?" my father asked.

"Computer science, Papa. That is something which I am very much interested in."

"Haan, but I think you must opt for electronics and telecommunication. You can get into the IT stream and the telecom line will always be open for you," he suggested.

"But I don't like electronics. I will take up computers and will work to build computer games later," I replied.

But he persisted, "Telecom is an emerging stream nowadays. I heard in BBC news last night that India will be the biggest market for mobiles in the coming years. Think about the future, not the present. You must take electronics and telecom, no other option."

I heard him but was determined, "No Papa, let me do what interests me. I will only take computer science in whichever college or city I choose."

While we were discussing this, one of the peons announced five roll numbers to proceed to room five; mine was one of them.

I touched my parent's feet, and they wished me best of luck from outside, as from here it was me who'd take the decisions. I felt grown up all of a sudden.

I entered room number five and saw one old man wearing a white shirt with big glasses over his eyes. This was a room which decided who were going to be the future engineers of this nation. In front of me stood one girl wearing a salwar suit with a flower print, oily hair, and small earrings twinkling in the white tube light. She looked tense. Holding an enrollment form in her hand, she had rolled it into multiple folds and was crushing it with her hands in tension. I heard her saying, "Oh god, what will happen?"

Looking at her, I forgot my own nervousness and prayed, "*Oh god, please give her whichever college and branch she desires.*"

The guy with the first number chose his college and moved to the next seat to submit his form. I was fourth in line now, and she was third. She was trying to lean in front to listen to what the others were opting for.

I was sure I'd take computer science, whichever college or city was available. As I stood behind her, I saw one pigeon sitting on the top of the ceiling window and his neck was moving in the same direction as her feet.

As we inched closer to our turn, the girl kept jostling forward.

"Can you please stand still and wait for your turn?" the counsellor asked her strictly.

She hid her face with the form she was holding and replied softly, "Sorry sir."

It was her turn and she moved to the counter and forwarded the crushed form to the counsellor. "What is this? Look at the state of the form," he chided.

She said sorry again and asked for RK College of Engineering, Jabalpur. The counsellor asked which branch she wanted, and she replied electronics and telecommunication.

The counsellor looked at the sheet in front for him and then filled the college name and branch in her form and signed and made an entry in his diary.

Now it was my chance to prod. I asked her bringing my face near her, "Which branch and college did you take?"

She turned to me and looked into my eyes, "Electronics and Telecom, RK Jabalpur." And something moved in my heart. It felt like someone had shaken me hard. The ugly room looked beautiful but I was still sure I wanted to opt for computer science.

I thanked her and proceeded to the counsellor.

"Which branch… college?" he asked me taking my form.

"Electronics and Telecommunication, RK, Jabalpur," I replied.

Something had happened. That one look changed my decision, which even my father had not been able to for days. Was I doing the right thing? Why was I opting for electronics? Just because of her? No ways, because this is fine. My father had advised the same, I tried to console myself. But I knew it was not my father, it was something different, which even I didn't know then.

My mind stopped working, my eyes stopped blinking, my heartbeat became normal, and my sweat dried off when the counsellor filled branch and college in my form, signed off and asked me to move to another seat.

I collected my form and moved to the next seat, but my eyes were looking for her. I turned left, right and then around, but could not find her in the room.

"Give me your form, give me your form," the person taking care of the next round of formalities said.

"Oh! Sorry, here it is." I handed over my form and after completing the formalities, I went outside and found my parents waiting for the result. I felt like a warrior returning from a long battle and my parents waiting to greet me, their eyes filled with love.

"So, which college did you choose? Bhilai one?" my father asked me anxiously, while my mom was already in tears.

"RK, Jabalpur," I replied softly and then continued looking at my father. "Electronics and telecommunication."

My father looked shocked.

"But you wanted to opt for computer science, you said?"

"Han! But then your face came in front of my eyes and I changed my mind to electronics and telecommunication. You are my father and you know what's best for me," I replied with an innocent face and bent down to touch his feet. He smiled and patted my back.

Well, the reason was definitely something else or rather someone else. But I was a committed man towards Navya and she would be waiting for me, so guess this was nothing more than an infatuation.

I tried to ignore her voice, I tried to ignore her twinkling earrings, but something in her eyes had made me follow her to Jabalpur.

While we were returning home in a local bus, I was wondering if I'd recognize her when I would reach college. What was her name? Would she be my friend? But then, I shook my head.

"*Oh Rohan! Please concentrate on Navya. You have been in love with her for the past three years. She is the only one for you. Do not get distracted by minor benefits.*"

I tried thinking about Navya, but was more confused about why an unknown girl had left such an impact on my thoughts. I was delighted that day and wanted to rush home and hug my sister. I wanted to eat all my favourite dishes before leaving for Jabalpur. The 16th of June was the date when I was supposed to join. I'd miss my parents and Surbhi Di, but change, they say, is the only constant.

I had never been left alone or travelled alone. This would be a new experience for me, living far away from home with friends in a hostel. I hoped this would be a new chapter in my life, which would unfold many hidden truths about myself.

I was all set to board the bus to Jabalpur with five pairs of shirts, five sets of trousers, a cotton mattress and a pillow, and of course my suitcase for my personal stuff. It was mentioned in the college guidelines that new students would not be allowed to wear jeans and t-shirts, which I wasn't happy about.

My mom sighed and Surbhi Di hugged me as I left for the bus stop to catch the morning bus. Papa had come along, not speaking much. He'd miss me, I knew, but I was leaving for my good and this was part of life.

We boarded the bus which was overcrowded and took the front seat. As the bus moved, I glanced at the city as if I would never return. *"Bye bye Navya, I am going far from you, so that I can return to you soon."*

I was happy and scared. I looked outside the window while my father took the seat next to me. It was the month of June and the hot air from the window was uncomfortable, to say the least. But we'd have to bear the five-hour-long journey.

I tried to push the window shut as my father doled out advice.

"Be a good boy in college, concentrate on your studies. We will not be there to keep an eye on you. You will be under your own care from now. Life is tough, and it's your determination and effort which will bring change to your life. You must call every Sunday and talk to your mom. Students enter college politics, so please a keep safe distance from such anti-social elements. Never drink and smoke. And yes, I will miss you a lot," he added softly.

I held his hand and assured him that I'd follow his advice.

We reached Jabalpur around one in the afternoon. We had lunch in a local hotel at the bus stop in Damoh Naka and then took a rickshaw to reach Jabalpur Cantonment where my college was.

I stood in front of the college gate, painted blue with white stripes and on top of which was written 'RK College of Engineering, Jabalpur'.

On both sides of the gate were tall eucalyptus trees standing in a row. Being a cantonment area, it was beautiful, neat and clean. My eyes rested on nearby *pan khokha,* where few boys were watching us with cigarettes in their hands. Definitely a corner to hang out and pass time. It was scorching hot and I pulled out my napkin and cleaned my face.

I was wearing a black and brown checked shirt, black pants and was carrying a small school bag on my back. Papa took a sip from bottle he was carrying and we proceeded inside the campus. The campus was full of tall trees, under the shade of which students were sitting and chatting. I was sure they were seniors. To my left, I could see a big shaded room. It was probably a lab as I could hear the sound of machines coming from it. A pale yellow coloured building in front was the main building I suppose, and we went towards it. As we reached the building, we could see some classes going on.

To my right, I could see a big ground where some of the seniors where playing cricket. We got inside the building and saw a few boys and girls standing near one room.

"They look like freshers as they are also wearing formals and standing quietly with their parents. Let's go," Papa observed.

We reached the room and I stood near the wall while Papa went inside to enquire. Next to me stood a tall boy. He looked at me, smiled and asked, "Fresher?"

I smiled too and replied as I was sure he was one, "Yes and you?"

He looked towards the room and then replied, "Your senior. Be prepared for a meeting tonight in the hostel, and yes, do not wear underwear with any holes."

I got goose bumps in a second. My eyes opened wide, so did my mouth. I looked down. Papa came out along with the hostel warden from the room before he could interrogate me further.

"Hello Rohan, how are you? I am your warden Rana. Come, I will take you to the hostel," Rana, my hostel warden who was an ex-Army man, spoke with enthusiasm and energy.

My hostel was not in the college campus but nearby at Russel Chowk, about two kilometres from the campus. Being a private college which was still under construction, they had converted a three-star hotel into a hostel.

The warden took his Bajaj scooter and instructed the rickshaw driver to follow him to the Maruti Hotel, Russel Chowk.

I smiled and looked around with interest. This was the area where I would spend the next four years of my life.

As we reached outside Maruti Hotel, we saw the warden standing there. Papa paid the rickshaw driver while I pulled out my suitcase and other luggage.

The warden called a boy named Chhotu, who was a peon in the hostel to carry my luggage and asked him to keep them in room number 107. He then showed us around the hostel. He first took us to the ground floor.

"Here is the reception, STD booth and pool table."

My eyes rested on a tall, heavily-built senior, with a cigarette in his hands, playing pool. He too looked at me, like a tiger looks at an innocent lamb.

He then took us to the first floor, taking the side stairs made up of wood. He shouted at Chhotu. "Why has the light not been replaced here? It's so dark, change it now!"

My father was happy to see that the warden was so caring. He told me, "It's good, you can call us from the STD booth below."

Rana sir took us to the first floor and continued the tour, "The first floor is for new students and my room is also on the same floor. I ensure that new students are kept safe from ragging. The second and third floors are for seniors and the RO water purifier is on the second floor from which students can fill clean water."

He then opened the door of room number 107. "This is your room. One more student Akash will share this room with you. He is still in college, completing formalities. I guess he will join you in the evening as his stuff is at his relative's place."

It was an amazing room – with no walls. With no walls, I mean, no wall was visible. They were completely covered with pictures of girls, models, film actresses – nude and semi-nude. It had a double bed in the centre, a small dressing table and two study tables placed at the corners.

My father looked around uncomfortably as I looked down.

"Remove these pictures once you settle down," he said and I nodded.

The warden handed over the keys to me and asked me to be comfortable, and to call him if I needed anything. While he was speaking, someone began singing loudly in the corridor. The warden opened the door and shouted his name.

"He is one of your seniors, Daman Shrivastava."

I said hello to him and shook hands with him. Daman touched my father's feet. "Uncle, don't worry, he is Rohan Verma and I am Shrivastava, we are both Kayastha. I will take care of him. He is like my younger brother."

Papa patted his back and thanked him. Daman had curly hair and was rather shabby. He smiled at me and I reciprocated. I was happy to find someone so helpful. He then took our leave.

The warden also left and we got down to arranging the room. As everyone left my room, Papa asked me to sit down. He pulled out a chair and sat in front of me.

"I will not say anything much. You are a big boy now and we have a lot of expectations from you. From here onwards, you are responsible for yourself. Keep yourself safe and do not indulge in any anti-social activities. Study hard and make your future bright."

He then helped me arrange my stuff. It was already five by the time we were done. Papa had his bus at six and he needed to leave.

I went downstairs with him to see him off. He looked sad and so did I. I touched his feet and he hugged me. I could see tears in his eyes. I was also crying, and my heart was heavy. I hugged him again, and he got into an auto and left.

I kept looking at him till the auto left my sight. I returned to my room. By this time, most of the seniors had returned from college and there was a lot of noise. I pulled out my keys and opened my room, but before I could enter, a fat tall boy entered pushing past me.

"Oh bhai, fresher?" he asked. I knew the basic rules of ragging and I knew I must not look into the senior's eyes. I looked down and replied, "Yes, sir."

"Bhai, my name is Vineet, from Devas. I am also a fresher, bhai. Cool down."

I relaxed. He looked like the father of two kids. We hugged each other, exchanged our names, and he took over my bed. "Your room is amazing bhai, so many sexy girls. I am not going anywhere," he said looking around.

"But I need to get rid of them. Papa asked me to."

"*Pagal ho gaya hai kya?* These will make your future, didn't your father tell you? He must have also enjoyed it during his time," he replied in astonishment.

Soon, more students from the other rooms came into my room and my room got a new name that day – '*Blue Room*'.

I was having fun listening to their jokes and the leg pulling. Within a few minutes, it felt like we had been friends for ages.

Soon the warden came to our floor and took us to the terrace where we had our canteen. He asked us to have dinner early as there would be an introduction session with the seniors at night.

It seemed perfect – the warden introducing us to the seniors, with no scope for ragging. Tasty food was made that day and all the juniors laughed, chatted and ate together.

It was 9 p.m. Akash, my room-mate, had not yet arrived from his relative's house when the voice of the warden echoed on our floor.

"All the juniors, please come out!" He banged on the doors while shouting for us to come out.

We hurriedly came out from our rooms and gathered in the corridor. We were around twenty odd juniors on that floor. The corridor lights were turned on by then, with some corners still in darkness due to fused bulbs.

"Now it's time for your introduction to your seniors. Think of them as your parents for the next four years, learn from them as tomorrow you will become seniors yourselves. You need to respect them just like you respect your parents. They will help you in the best way they can," he briefed us and asked us to go to the fourth-floor recreation hall. We lined up and proceeded, fearing we were going to be ragged.

"The day has come for which I was waiting since a long time," Vineet replied grinning.

"Are you mad or what? They will rag us," I said in fear.

"Dost, remember, everyone gets ragged and it's part of engineering college. If you enjoy, it will go easy. So chill and do whatever they tell you to. Remove your clothes even before they ask you to."

As we reached the recreation room, there were around forty seniors standing like hungry dogs. We moved in and lined up against a wall.

While entering, I saw the same tall senior whom I had met in the morning in college. But why he was standing all naked between the others, wearing only his red underwear?

Before leaving, the warden briefed the seniors "Guys, you all are responsible boys now, do whatever you want, but ensure that no one gets hurts."

He spoke this and left the room, handing us over to the hungry dogs.

As he left, all the seniors came towards us. Daman sir, whom I had met in the afternoon, came towards me. I felt relaxed as he had assured Papa that he would take care of me.

He reached me, and gave me a tight slap. It was so hard that for seconds I couldn't hear anything. And then he spoke, "This was for shaking hands with me in the afternoon. Don't you know I am your senior and you can't even look at me!"

I said I was sorry, but I got another slap. "Juniors must speak only when asked to," he said.

This slap was on the other cheek and was much harder. Even my father had never slapped me so hard.

He kept looking at me when another senior took over, "Tell me your name."

I hesitated to speak up, but then replied, "Rohan, sir."

He pulled his hand back and slapped me tight, "Don't you have a surname?"

My eyes were filled with tears, but I fought them, "Rohan Verma."

He again pulled his hand back, gave me another tight slap, "You don't have a father, mother f**k**? Who will add his name in between?"

I replied, "Rohan Vijay Verma."

Hearing this, he gave me one more slap, "Who will add 'sir'?"

I replied, "Rohan Vijay Verma sir." He gave me one more tight slap, saying "Did I ask you to repeat yourself?"

But this last one was not so hard, or my cheeks had stopped sensing them by then perhaps.

The slaps continued for one hour, till all the forty seniors introduced themselves. I got around a hundred and twenty slaps by then. There was no sensation left on my cheeks.

It was already 10:30 p.m. by then, when one of the seniors shouted,

"Everyone listen, now enough of introductions. Some action time now. This boy standing naked in between is Akash, but for you, he is your dream girl. He will walk from this room to the ground floor, and you all need to follow her like you're walking on a ramp and then return to the same place. The condition is that while you walk, you have to strip, so by the time you are back to this room, your body must not have any clothes left on it."

I was shocked to hear that I'd have to strip. And even more to learn that the tall guy who was naked was Akash my roommate, who had tried to rag me in college. Tables had turned now and it was he who was shivering in fear.

"Start walking!" a senior shouted.

Akash started walking like a model on the ramp and we followed him. Vineet was enjoying the most; he pulled off all his clothes even before starting the walk. His pride was hanging for all to appraise. Seniors were hooting at us standing on both sides of the corridor.

We started our walk, stripping as we went along. By the time we reached the ground floor, some of us were semi-naked.

Vineet was completely naked, but the smile on his face showed how much he loved it.

We moved back, stripping to loud shouts, comments, and whistles from the seniors, motivating us to perform our best. Our clothes were all over the floors and I wondered if I'd ever be able to retrieve them.

We returned to the recreation room, and stood in a line, butt naked – our glory, our pride hanging like unwanted mangoes.

Akash stood next to me. I took a chance and poked my finger into his waist "Oh dream girl, how are you feeling now?"

He smiled and replied, "Sorry for the morning yaar." I smiled back forgiving him.

This session continued till three in the morning. We learned sexy poems, some rules to greet seniors and multiple other tasks, but one which was the best among them was to keep a condom as an identity card for the hostel. According to our branches, we got different brands of condoms, which we had to keep in our pockets all the time. If we failed to show it when asked, we'd have to wash the senior's clothes the entire week.

After a comic hunt for our clothes through the floors, we were finally set free. I finally got to know what ragging was. I had experienced it first hand and had rather enjoyed it despite the humiliation. When I returned to the blue room, I found Akash standing in front of the mirror.

"Hey Akash, what happened?"

"Minimum two hundred slaps," he replied.

I sat on the bed and replied,"Relax; this was just a trailer. We have six months to go."

"What are you saying man? My pride is not for these jerks," he replied, and we laughed.

Vineet then banged on our door and came in. Saying nothing, he climbed on the bed and lay down between us.

"What happened Vineet? This is not your room," I informed him

"After the torture, I want to sleep with these beautiful girls around me. You both also go to sleep and let me sleep as well. We have a class at 8:30 in the morning," he replied in sleep mode.

I smiled, hugged him and went to sleep.

This was how my first day at the hostel went, amazing, full of fun, making friends for life –Vineet and Akash.

I went to bed pondering. "*Mom, Papa, today your son has grown up. Today, I didn't come crying to you when I got hurt. Today, I made new friends; today, I learned tolerance; today, I realized what pressure is.*"

I thought about Navya as well. "*You made me strong Navya, your love made me do what I did today. Every slap I bore was because of the strength of your love within me. I love you more today, goodnight.*"

When I woke up the next morning, Vineet had taken over the bed. Akash was squeezed against the side wall, and I was dying with the weight of Vineet' s hand and legs on me. I managed to wriggle out and give one tight slap to Vineet. He woke up in shock, thinking the seniors had come in.

"Wake up Motu, it's college time!" I shouted at both.

We all got ready in our new college uniform for first-year students – sky blue shirts, black trousers and black formal shoes. We reached the ground floor and walked to college which was two kilometres from our hostel.

The juniors walked together towards college in a group, discussing the previous night. After twenty minutes, we were at our college gates. We parted to our different classes. Vineet was also from electronics and communication, and we both walked together to our class, which was on the first floor.

As we reached the door of the classroom, I saw *her!*

Wearing a sky blue kurti and white pajamas, her hair oiled and tied in two braids with red ribbons and wearing flat slippers, she was standing on a desk, dancing to "*Yaire… Yaire… zor laga ke nache re…*"

The other students were singing, crowding around her. She was moving her hands up and down, as Urmila had done in *Rangeela*.

41

She was smiling and enjoying herself as her eyes mirrored her confidence.

I stood at the door and kept watching, with a smile on my face. She was the same girl who had made me drop my plan of pursuing computer science in St. Joseph, Bhilai.

"What a scene is this! I am in love with her at first sight," Vineet spoke, looking at her with wide open eyes.

He pushed me with his hands, and I moved inside dancing in Amitabh Bachchan style, unaware that a few seniors were standing inside making her dance on the desk.

As I went on making my moves, everyone stood still. I glanced at her; she had also stopped dancing, and was smiling at me. The dimples on her cheeks reminded me of Navya. Then a voice said, "Oh hero! You want to dance?" One of our seniors Manjula Ranjan, was sitting on the teacher's desk, with three more seniors along. She jumped down from the desk.

She came close while I kept my eyes down.

"You have so much energy to be able to dance in front of seniors. What do you drink? Milk?" she asked me coming as close as possible as all the other seniors laughed aloud.

"C'mon, now you will sing, and she will dance," she said and returned to the desk.

I forgot to tell you all; I am a fantastic singer.

I gave my bag to Vineet, who was standing next to me, more interested in observing Manjula Ranjan.

I started with a song from movie the *Bombay.*

"*Tuhi re… tuhi re… tere bina mae kaise…*"

And Manjula interrupted me. She looked at the girl standing on the desk and said, "Oh madam, you need to dance."

She made a face. Who can dance to such a slow and sad song. Anyway, I started again, and she made a few moves with her hand. She still looked beautiful, moving her hands up and down. The seniors were laughing at her, while I was singing loud. My voice could be heard outside the class.

Someone entered the classroom and the seniors stood up hastily. Everyone stood still, except me, who was still singing loudly.

"Do you need a special invitation to stop singing?" A stern voice scolded me.

She was our Physics subject teacher, Priti ma'am.

The seniors greeted her and left the class. We all took our seats. I pulled my bag from Vineet' s hand.

Priti ma'am placed her books on the front desk and introduced herself. "I am Priti and will take your Physics classes in the first semester. This subject also has sessionals involved, so do not mess-up in my class."

She looked at all of us and continued, "As you all are new, one by one, you can introduce yourselves, starting from that corner."

Vineet was the first one to start, "Good morning friends, I am Vineet Sinha from Devas, studied in DAV Public School and living in a hostel here."

"Hi, I am Tavish from Rewa. Studied in Bal Vidya Mandir and residing in Jabalpur at my uncle's house."

I was looking down and paying attention to each introduction. These were the people with whom I would spend four years of my life. Suddenly I heard a familiar voice, "Hi ma'am, I am Vaidehi Sharma from Jabalpur. Completed my schooling from Christ Church Girls Senior Secondary School. I am a passionate person, who loves to explore and travel."

As I heard her introduction, I realized I was sitting next to her. In a rush to take seats, I had sat down next to her unknowingly. I moved my head up and looked at her, "*Vaidehi. What a name!*"

My turn came, and I stood up and started my introduction. "I am Rohan Verma from Sagar and completed my schooling from St. Joseph Convent School."

As I sat down, she looked at me and smiled. "How come Convent School? It's a girl's school," she asked me smiling.

I turned towards her and replied, so that ma'am could not hear, "It's co-ed in Sagar. By the way, I am Rohan and you..."

She again smiled, "Why didn't you listen to my name when I introduced myself?"

Before I could answer, ma'am shouted "You both, can you please stop? There are others in your class who are still introducing themselves."

We stopped talking.

While the introduction of the sixty-odd students continued, she pulled her pen out and wrote something on a notebook in front of her and turned it towards me. I pulled her notebook towards myself.

You sing well. Impressed.

I looked at her eyes, she was smiling. I thanked her with my eyes and then pulled out my pen to reply:

And you dance fabulously.

She smiled back and again wrote something and pushed her notebook to me.

Would you mind singing for me in the break?

I smiled, biting my lips and then replied writing,

How will I get paid?

She read it and gave an angry look and wrote back:

Zyada bhav mat kha.

She pulled the notebook before I could even read it, wrote something else and passed it to me.

You are a hosteller. I can share my tiffin daily. My mom makes delicious food.

I smiled and replied:

This is an exciting offer. I can sing three times a day, please bring lunch and dinner too.

She smiled and slapped me on my shoulder.

While we were interacting, hiding from Priti ma'am, we forgot, there were sixty more eyes in class who were observing us. Vineet and a close friend of Vaidehi, Chaaru, were among those.

Once Ptiti ma'am's lecture was over, we stood up to move out of class. I looked at her, smiled and said, "You have a nice name – Vaidehi."

"Don't expect me to say that you have a good name too." She made a face at me, picked up her books, and left holding Chaaru's hand.

I smiled at her attitude and turned to look for Vineet, who was staring at me with a funny smile.

"First day setting, *maan gaye,* Rohan boss," he said punching me on my back.

We picked our bags, and as we were going outside, one interesting fellow tried entering the class, holding a helmet in his left hand, bag on his back, sweating profusely.

"Oh! Is the class over?" he asked me, pulling out his spectacles to clean.

"Bhai, you are too for this late or too early for the next class."

"I got stuck ya. My mama took me to Bada Phuara (a very congested market in Jabalpur) and because of him, I got f**ked today. I am Anurag Thakur," he said with a frown.

"Chill bhai, nothing much happened except introductions. I am Rohan, and he is Motu, sorry Vineet," I assured him.

He pulled out his handkerchief to clean his face. We shook hands, and all three of us went to the canteen before the next class started.

On our way, I asked Anurag, "Are you from Jabalpur or staying at some relative's house?"

"Na re, I am from Jabalpur. From Model School," he replied.

We reached the canteen. Vineet sat down quietly. I ordered samosas for the three of us and asked Vineet. "What happened Motu? So sad? *Ghar ki yaad aa rahi hai kya?*"

Vineet picked up a samosa and replied, "No yaar, I am in love. I cannot forget her beautiful face."

I hit his back and laughed, "And who is that unlucky girl?"

"Priti ma'am bey. She is just so beautiful. How do I propose to her?" Motu replied poetically.

"*Lo, ye to pehle din hi gaye kaam se.* Grow up man, stop staring at ma'am now. There are so many girls all around," Thakur replied in his style.

Motu came closer to Thakur's face. "Whom do you want me to stare at? Vaidehi, who is sitting behind you and making gestures at Rohan."

I was shocked and instinctively pulled my samosa out on hearing that Vineet had observed both of us.

As we reached the canteen, I had seen her sitting there. She gestured with her eyes for me to sit next to her in the next class too and I confirmed with my eyes as well.

"Nothing like that, yaar. She smiled, and so I smiled back, that's all," I replied.

Motu now turned his face with attitude while I could still see her giggling with her friends. "Okay then, in the next class, you must sit with me, and then it will be proved."

Thakur nodded in agreement. Though I too wanted to sit with her, I wanted to prove these two jerks wrong and so decided to sit with them.

Break time was over, and we returned to our classroom on the first floor. Our engineering drawing sir entered the classroom, and we all followed him in.

Vaidehi was moving in front of me, along with Chaaru. Vineet waited to see what I would do. Vaidehi moved to the first-row seat, turned and looked at me. Chaaru, who was with her, moved to sit next to her, but she stopped her and asked her to come in from the other side.

Vaidehi moved inside the bench. She showed me the space next to her. But I couldn't let Motu and Thakur talk about this in the hostel, so I ignored her and sat with Motu, in the same row, but on the other side of the room.

She stopped smiling; her dimples were gone. She pulled her chair and settled down, looking in front.

She turned towards me once, without smiling, pulled the pen cap off in anger and wrote something in her notebook.

Thakur who was sitting next to me scolded Motu. "*Sale, tere karan,* she is angry with him now."

I was enjoying the way they were teasing me.

I turned towards her again, to check if she was observing me, but she was looking in front. I too concentrated what our teacher was explaining, but my mind went back to the past. A similar thing had happened with Navya and me once.

It was a time when we had the annual function in our school. I performed in two group dances, in which Navya was also taking part. I participated only because of her, even though all my friends were busy with the preparation for the twelfth board exams.

Parents and outsiders were invited to the show which started at five in the evening and finished by nine. As students, we used to be very excited for it, as it was the only day when we got to stay so long in school.

We were waiting backstage for our performance. It was a cold evening in the month of December. Navya was looking fabulous in a black sari, which she wore for the performance. It was great seeing her in a black sari printed with golden flowers, as I had always seen her only in the school uniform.

She was looking gorgeous with make-up and a different hairstyle. We were standing behind the stage entrance, which faced the park of our school.

She was standing near me, along with some of her friends. Sonal was one of them.

"The moon is so bright," I showed her. She looked up and smiled.

"You like it?" she asked me in soft voice.

Though she was looking at the moon, I was watching her and replied, "Yes, it's beautiful." She knew what I was talking about, but feigned ignorance. Sonal was smiling at my words though.

"I am so tired standing… how much longer do we have to wait?" Navya said in frustration.

I couldn't let her feel tired. I had to find a solution. I looked here and there and saw the stairs. I went there, pulled out my handkerchief and cleaned the steps. She was staring at me anxiously, while Sonal was smiling.

I sat there first, Navya turned her face and spoke to Sonal. I gesture to her to come and sit next to me so that she could be comfortable. She looked at me, smiled, and then Sonal came smiling towards me, "Thanks a lot Rohan. I was so tired standing."

I gestured in anger to Navya, while she smiled, hiding her face behind a pillar. I still remember how beautiful she looked that day. I understood, she was playing games with me. I stood back and went to her, and spoke coming closer to her, "If you are standing, how can I sit?"

She turned and moved forward towards the stage, stopped after a few steps later and turned back. "Our performance is about to start, will you come or keep standing there?"

I smiled and rushed towards the stage. We performed excellently that day.

Thakur tapped at my hand, "Rohan *beta,* stop sleeping. The class is almost over."

I was sleeping in class, dreaming about Navya. I was really exhausted after the night's ragging session.

As the class got over, we stood up from our seats pandiculating. I saw Vaidehi moving out without looking at me. I threw my bag to Thakur and rushed to follow her; she was walking fast with Chaaru, holding her books in her hand.

I shouted her name to stop her. "Vaidehi, wait!"

Chaaru turned to look, but Vaidehi continued walking.

I ran towards them, "Hey Vaidehi, listen please."

She stopped, turned towards me and said, "Yes, Rohan?"

I caught my breath, "Sorry, I sat with Vineet."

She kept looking at me indifferently and said, "So?"

"You wanted me to... but Vineet forced..." I stammered.

"You got me wrong," she clarified and left with Chaaru.

I was sure she had wanted me to sit with her, but instead I had received quite a bit of her attitude.

Thakur came behind me with my bag, "She is Vaidehi from Christ Church, famous for her attitude in most of the schools of Jabalpur."

I looked at Thakur, held his neck and asked, "Who told you, your mama?"

We smiled, laughed and ran towards the gate. It was a hot sunny afternoon and we had ice cream outside the college gate. I then saw Vaidehi walking with books in her hand and a bag on her back, to the other side of college.

"Where is she going?" I asked Thakur.

"She lives nearby in Gorakhpur colony, behind the Gurdwara. Guess she is walking back," he replied.

After the first day of college, Thakur – who was from Jabalpur – urged us to come with him to Gwarighat to see the famous Hanuman temple.

Gwarighat is located on the banks of river Narmada, famous for various temples and pilgrimage sites.

Vineet and I rode pillion on Thakur's scooter. It was tough to adjust with two heavyweights, and I felt like the cheese between a bun. But our outing was fantastic, and we appreciated the beauty of Jabalpur in the evening.

We visited the Hanuman temple and prayed. The cold air blew around us after colliding with the river currents. The sound of water was stupefying. The *arti* at the ghat was fantastic. We bought some peanuts and sat on the steps of the ghat.

Vineet pulled out his cigarette and lit it.

"It was a beautiful day, wasn't it?" I spoke feeling calm.

Vineet took a few puffs and so did Thakur.

"The day was beautiful, or Vaidehi was wonderful?" asked Vineet.

I looked at the river deep in thoughts and replied, "I am already committed; I have a girlfriend."

Vineet pulled in the smoke and coughed in shock. "What? Great, so you have one girlfriend and want another here?"

"No yaar, I was just trying to be friendly with her," I replied.

Thakur, who had been listening quietly, spoke, "I too loved her once, but even being her friend is a tough task."

Vineet and I turned towards him, "You came late to college, when did all that happen?"

Thakur, making a sad face, said, "It's a long story man."

"And we have all the time to listen to it," I replied.

Thakur stood up, faced us, took a cigarette from Vineet and took four to five puffs in one go.

"I proposed to her in my tenth standard. I bought a friendship card for her after school, waited outside her school and tried giving it to her when she was boarding her school bus."

He paused as we waited expectantly. He took a few more puffs. "Then what happened?"

He looked at me sadly, took one more puff and replied, "Nothing, she tore it up and one of her school teachers sent a complaint to my school."

I laughed aloud. "Oh my, you were rejected by her, poor Thakur."

Vineet too was laughing, but was more worried about his cigarette that Thakur wasn't returning.

"But why are you excited dear? She will dump you one day," Thakur replied.

"She didn't dump you, she kicked you. But you still don't understand," Vineet teased him.

Thakur beat him in jest while Vineet ran across the ghat. We cherished those moments and then later in the evening, Thakur dropped us back to our hostel.

"Why don't you come up to our room?" Vineet asked Thakur.

Thakur agreed and we told him about our seniors and the rules juniors had to follow.

"No problem. I have many contacts in Jabalpur, no one can even touch me," Thakur replied in confidence and pulled his scooter on the stand and followed us upstairs.

After a few minutes, we were sitting in my room with six seniors and our dear Anurag Thakur, the pride of Jabalpur, was dancing in his underwear to '*Nimbuda Nimbuda Nimbuda...*' a song from the movie *Hum Dil De Chuke Sanam*.

He was allowed to leave after his fantastic dance performance. He was looking at us in anger, while we were laughing loudly.

"Don't you dare tell anyone in college about this," he said while kicking his scooter.

As he left, I crossed the road and moved to the other side of my hostel, where there was a bakery.

I asked for some patties and saw one of my seniors, Neeraj was standing there, smoking a cigarette. As I was paying for the patties, he came close to me. He was tall and handsome, and belonged to Delhi. He was the only person who hadn't slapped us even once. He seemed the most decent among the seniors. His branded clothes were proof that he belonged to a wealthy family. We had heard he was so rich that he used to give his underwear to the laundry.

"Saw you with Vaidehi in college. You both were sitting together," he came close and said.

I greeted him and turned my face down to my third button as per rule.

"Relax, look up!"

I felt better, thanked him and ate my patties and replied, "Yes sir, but that was the only seat available."

He listened and then said, "She is exquisite. I liked her in the first instance."

Oh god. Why was everyone going crazy about her? She was just an ordinary girl, except maybe her attitude. But by then, I was unaware that she had started building a house in my heart in some corner.

We conversed for sometime and he asked questions about my family and hobbies. I returned to my room soon after.

It is a done thing that engineers wake up at night. When it is midnight, we all wake up; our eyes become fresh, songs turn on in various rooms, and you can hear boys running and chatting in each room. It was like the morning for us.

I was going through my semester books when Akash called me out of the room to come to the terrace where Vineet and Anna were also waiting.

Anna was from the south. Though his name was Rama Lingam Kulati Ieyar, we called him Anna. He was a chain smoker and gave Vineet good company.

As we reached, I saw Vineet and Anna, peeping at the roadside wall, which goes towards Jyoti Talkies. Jyoti Talkies was one of the most famous cinema houses of Jabalpur and was close to our hostel.

"What are you all doing here? Why have you called me?" I asked.

"Every Thursday night, people from Jyoti Talkies come to paste big movie posters on that wall," Anna replied.

I was confused and asked him making a face, "So what?"

"Today is Thursday and the movie *Taal* is releasing tomorrow. They will come to stick its poster. And I love Aishwarya Rai," Anna replied pulling out a cigarette.

I finally understood. They were planning to steal the movie poster that would be pasted on the wall in a while.

I pulled up the bench with the help of Akash and sat in front of Vineet and Anna. He took one puff and forwarded his cigarette to me. I declined.

"Arrey bhai, try it. You will look dashing," Anna told me.

I looked at Anna, who was dark, short, and thin with wispy hair. "Well, you certainly look dashing after smoking twenty-four hours!"

We all laughed, and I continued, "I will never smoke, no matter what happens."

"What if your girlfriend leaves you?" Anna asked me.

I looked at him with wistful eyes, thinking about Navya. Would someday Navya lead me to this stage that I would smoke?

Vineet interrupted my thoughts. "Rohan, how did you meet your school girlfriend and what is her name?"

"Oh! So, you had a girlfriend?" Anna and Akash made a funny face to tease me.

I smiled and folded my legs on that bench, looked at the clear sky twinkling with bright stars.

I started.

"At the beginning of the twelfth standard, my school appoints office bearers during the commencement of the session. Twelve different portfolios to manage in school, for which teachers select a captain from twelfth standard and a vice-captain from the eleventh standard.

It was Monday morning when one of my friends informed me that office bearers list was up on the school notice board and my name was on it. I rushed to the notice board to find my name posted as Discipline Minister and Navya as Deputy Discipline Minister. I didn't know who she was so I asked one of my friends, and he only told me 'Lucky you are!'

It was assembly time, and all the classes were lined up. I was standing in front of the stage on which our principal was standing. She was a nun from the missionary of St. Joseph. She would announce the names of the ministers and captains of the school for that year and would introduce us to all the students. Once the morning prayers were over, she came in front and informed us that office bearers had been chosen and as she would announce the name, the students had to come on stage to give their introduction.

She called my name first, "Rohan Verma, Discipline Minister." I moved out from my class line and walked towards the stage while all the students clapped. I reached the stage, wished the principal and stood on one side. Then she took names of the other ministers one by one, and everyone came on stage and lined up starting from me. She first announced all the names from class twelfth and then started announcing the names of deputy ministers from class eleventh.

My eyes were waiting to see who Navya was. By then, I had only heard her name, but not seen her. I kept waiting for my principal to call out her name. Finally she did.

I could see a fair smiling face with dimples on the cheeks, blunt cut hair, excitement in the eyes move out from her class line hugging her close friends. Her purple hairband was so placed to not let a single hair come on her face. Neatly dressed with socks pulled up to her knees, she walked confidently to the stage. I didn't want to miss a single step she was taking and could only think that I was certainly a lucky boy.

She stood next to me, smiling, while I just looked at her dimples.

I was hungry but didn't want to eat, I was thirsty but didn't want to drink, my mind was not in control, my eyes were only seeing her everywhere. My heart was thinking only one thing: "Am I in love with her?"

I was becoming nostalgic narrating to my friends how I had met her, when Akash shouted.

"Bhaiyon, they have stuck the poster! Let's go."

We all stood up, forgetting my love story, and peeped from the terrace to confirm if Akash was correct. Yes, he was. "We must rush, before the gum dries off."

We ran towards the ground floor, following each other with Anna leading the show. Vineet pulled along a fiber chair so that we could climb on it and pull the poster out.

We rushed outside. Chhotu who was sleeping at the main door, walked away. He knew where we were heading. Soon we reached below the wall on which the poster was pasted, looked at it and discussed our plan of action.

Vineet placed the chair just below the poster and Akash being the tallest stood on it and, he pulled out the poster from the side.

"Careful with Aishwarya's face," Anna insisted, pulling out one more cigarette from his pocket.

"Why you smoke so much, Anna?" I slapped him on his head

"What to do? It's heredity," he replied.

I laughed. "What heredity?"

"My *baap* is a chain smoker, his father had a business of making bidis. I learned to smoke when I was thirteen years old, so it is hereditary. Now do you get it?" he explained.

I saluted him smiling when Akash spoke, "Hold this and let's move to the hostel fast."

We rushed towards the hostel and took it to Vineet's room. My room was already covered with models and girls and had no space for this big poster.

Vineet was excited to have Aishwarya in his room. Our other friends also came to his room to admire the new addition.

Vineet slept in his room that day. We all laughed and giggled before falling asleep.

Next morning, the weather was remarkably pleasant. Clouds had drifted over Jabalpur. It was the end of June. The monsoons would hit Jabalpur, making it pleasant.

We were about to reach the college gate when the rain started pouring. I along with Vineet, Akash and Anna ran towards the college entrance to take shelter. By the time we arrived at the canteen, we were drenched. I saw my other classmates standing in the lobby, enjoying the rain. The class had not started yet; maybe the teacher was late.

I asked Vineet to run towards the lobby with me and enjoy the rain with the others there. We both ran towards the lobby taking the stairs.

We were soaked in rainwater and as I reached, I shook my hair with my fingers, trying to dry them out.

I saw Vaidehi leaning on the boundary wall of the lobby. She was smiling, placing her hands out to touch the rainwater. The flowers on the ground floor garden were blooming in the first rains. I looked at her; she was looking beautiful. She had tied her hair perfectly, had put on a light pink lipstick and was wearing small golden earrings. Something was different. I observed later that her braids were missing and she had tied a ponytail with a pink rubber band, making her look gorgeous. She saw me as I reached upstairs; she turned towards me facing towards Chaaru, who was standing in front of her.

Vaidehi looked at me, and smiling, she spoke to Chaaru again. Then she played with a handkerchief in her hands while gesturing with her eyes. I understood; she was offering me her handkerchief which she was rotating around her fingers.

I smiled at her while shaking my hair to get them dry.

"Hello Chaaru, how are you?" I smiled and greeted Chaaru. Vaidehi turned back towards the wall to check the rain with a smiling face. She would not leave any stone unturned to show some attitude.

I leaned my back on the boundary wall next to Vaidehi. As I moved backward, I could see her face. She looked at me with her beautiful eyes and smiled.

I looked to the other side and then at her again. She was still staring at me, moving her handkerchief towards me. I lifted my hand to hold it and tried to take it from her. She kept looking at me, without releasing it, with a playful smile on her face. I looked into her eyes, she kept smiling and then released the handkerchief with a jerk.

"Thanks for this." I smiled and wiped my face.

"You don't have an umbrella or a raincoat?" she asked me smiling, ignoring Chaaru who went inside the classroom, feeling neglected.

I smiled back at her and replied, "Then how would you have given me your handkerchief?"

She placed her left hand on her waist, making a face, "Am I dying to give you my handkerchief?" and she pulled it back.

"Oh, sorry yaar, thanks for this." I took it back.

She was an attractive, intelligent and confident girl. And you could not flirt with her. She had all the rights reserved for that.

She turned looking at the rain and asked me, "Why didn't you sit with me?"

I replied after thinking for a second, "I thought you will not be talking with me anymore today."

"You didn't answer my question," she retorted with a pause.

What should I say? I thought for an instant, turned my face towards her, "I am sorry, let us sit together today." She smiled pulling her handkerchief back.

We went inside for the class.

We sat together, and I saw Vineet smiling along with Thakur.

Ma'am explained a physics theorem and as I was listening to the lecture, by mistake my feet touched Vaidehi's feet. I immediately reached for her hand and touched my forehead and softly said sorry.

"What was that?" she asked me

"I have been taught by my parents, that girls are a form of goddesses and must not be touched by the feet, and if touched by mistake, then one must touch her hand and touch your forehead – a way to say sorry," I explained, hiding from Priti ma'am.

I turned to concentrate on the lecture, but now Vaidehi was in the mood to flirt. Her feet touched my feet again; I thought it was by mistake and I again touched her hand and touched my forehead. She smiled and in the next three or four seconds, her feet again touched my feet. But this time, before I moved my hand to touch her, she forwarded her palm in front of me on the desk.

I again tried to concentrate, but my mind was on her, when her feet again touched me. I understood that she was doing it intentionally. She smiled and moved her palm again for me to touch. And I repeated the same, not revealing that I knew she was doing it intentionally. She did this every two to three minutes and smiled at me.

While we both were preoccupied in the touching game, Priti ma'am had noticed us. She stopped speaking, came to our seat and looking at me angrily, she said, "Can you please get out of the class?"

Listening to her, I stood up, said sorry, picked up my bag and moved out of the class, unaware that Vaidehi too had picked up her books and walked out behind me.

As I reached out, the rain had already stopped. I leaned on the boundary wall to check if it was still raining, taking my hands out. I thought I'd go to the canteen and join the next class, but as I turned, I was shocked to see Vaidehi standing behind me, with her head down. She looked at me with sad eyes.

"Why you are out? Did she send you out too?" I asked her in astonishment

She moved towards the stairs, without answering.

"She is really scary, but see how nice it is outside." I spoke, following her, while she started going down the stairs.

I continued, pulling my bag on my shoulders, "But how could she have sent you out? You are a studious girl."

She halted hearing me, turned towards me and looked at me. "Fool, she didn't turn me out. I came out for you."

She spoke in anger and ran down the stairs, leaving me standing alone.

Did she really do this? What guts she had! A girl coming out for a boy and ignoring the teacher in class. I smiled and ran towards her. She was still walking fast, towards the area outside the admin building.

I ran towards her and stopped her pulling her left hand from behind. She stopped and turned towards me. She was close to me; I could feel her breath. Her eyes stopped blinking. I held her hand softly, and she stepped back.

"You came out for me?" I asked her.

"Are you coming with me to the canteen?" she asked. I smiled and walked with her. As we took a few steps, she laughed and so did I.

"You really believe girls are goddesses or were you just trying to touch me?" she asked in a naughty tone.

I looked at her, thought for a while and asked her a different question, "Did your feet really touch mine accidentally or did you want me to touch your hand?"

She stopped walking, looked at me smiling with her hand on her waist. What a look she gave me.

"Can you ever give a straight answer?" she asked me back.

We walked again smiling.

"Will you be my friend?" she asked me looking down.

"Friends forever!" I replied. She smiled back, welcoming the new ray of friendship in between both of us.

I was happy to be her friend; she was an adorable, sweet girl, and I loved to be with her. We reached the canteen, and as we took a seat, she pulled out her tiffin.

"This is for you," she told me.

I opened it and saw *parathas, aloo sabji,* with some lemon pickle inside. The aroma reminded me of my mother's kitchen. Without waiting, I pulled out one *paratha* and ate with some *sabji.*

"Wow! Fantastic food. Every mother cooks so well, I suppose," I replied taking one big bite.

She was looking at me and smiling, with her cheek resting on her hand. I took another bite and asked her to eat too. She shook her head.

I closed her tiffin.

"Why don't you finish it?" she asked stopping my hands.

"Okay, but only if you eat along with me," I replied with the condition.

She made a weird face and took one small bite. I smiled and forced her to take a bigger one.

"Are you fussy about eating?" I asked her.

"I don't like eating at all," she replied making faces.

"Madam, try eating the hostel food for two days, and you will love everything your mother cooks."

While chatting away happily, we failed to notice that many students were observing the new chemistry between us.

"It's time for our mathematic class, let's go," she said closing the tiffin.

I leaned on a chair, pandiculating, "There are no sessionals for mathematics. I will not attend that class," I said.

She kept her books back on the table. "Well, even I am not interested in attending a class in such a pleasant weather," she said.

"So tell me something about your family?" she asked.

"It's Mom, Papa and my elder sister Surbhi. She is in college, doing her MA. And yours?" I questioned her back.

"Same. I have my Ma, Papa and my younger brother Dhruv. He is naughty, and is studying in class tenth."

I looked at her smiling, but my mind had shifted focus. I felt I had had a similar conversation with someone years ago. It began raining again. The sound of the rain falling on the canteen roof was loud. From the cafeteria window, I could see, the main road and cars moving drenched in rainwater.

My mind was going back to my memories when she interrupted me, "You are missing someone."

"No, no…" I shook my head, though.

She kept looking into my eyes, till I said, "Yes, actually I am not missing, but recalling something. Something similar happened years back."

She placed her books aside and asked, "A discussion between you and her?"

I looked at her moving my eyes from the window. "How do you know about her?"

"Mr Rohan, your eyes are saying everything. You have a girlfriend," she said, but didn't smile and her eyes were different.

"Navya is her name. She was my junior in school. It was raining that afternoon in the month of July. A few office bearers of my school had stayed after school to practice for our oath-taking ceremony," I replied.

"It was 3:30 p.m. We practiced our part a few times and then took a break. When I returned after drinking some water, I saw Navya weeping in a corner. The others hadn't returned to the auditorium yet.

"I was Discipline Minister, and Navya was Deputy Discipline Minister. We had just met two days back."

Vaidehi was listening to my story silently.

"I went to her, turning right and left to check if the others were coming inside. But there was no one. She saw me coming and tried to wipe away her tears, sitting on a small chair, which was used by the nursery students.

I went down on my knees and asked her if she was okay. She wiped her tears and said there was nothing to worry. I sat there for two more minutes to ensure she stopped crying. But when I saw she was still crying, I offered her my handkerchief. After wiping her tears, she said. 'It's tough if you don't have a mother.' I felt bad. She continued and told me, 'I live with my father and brother. My mom expired after the birth of my brother who is in class six now.' I interrupted her to ask if she was missing her mom. She said as she had not returned home on time today, her uncle had come to school and scolded her for not informing them about staying back.

"I consoled her and made her promise that she must stop shedding tears. After sometime, she smiled, then we laughed, practiced for our ceremony and became good friends from that day."

Vaidehi blinked her eyes, removing hands from her cheeks. "Navya, what a beautiful name. You love her a lot?" she asked.

I smiled and looked out of the window. I knew I loved Navya a lot, but something stopped me from confessing that to Vaidehi. What was stopping me, I wonder.

"I think we have to go to the practical room for our next class," I said instead.

She leaned back in her chair, "Oh god, this boy can never give a straight answer."

I smiled and asked her to get up. We walked outside while all the eyes of our seniors and our batch-mates in the canteen were on us. I could see them murmuring seeing us together in the college campus.

It was 1 a.m. on Saturday night when Anna came to our room and told us that they were going to the terrace to make some Maggi.

"Do you have Maggi? How will we cook? The mess is closed so there's no gas available," I asked him.

Anna leaned his shoulder on my door, lit a cigarette. "Where there is a will, there is a way," he responded in style.

I stood up from the bed. Akash was asleep, so we let him be.

I kicked Anna on his back and asked him to get going. As the days were passing, although we were still expected to respect our seniors, ragging had almost stopped, and we enjoyed their company as well.

As we reached the terrace, I saw that Vineet, Rahul and a few more guys had collected newspapers from all the rooms.

"What are you guys up to?" I asked, taking a seat, wearing my boxers and a t-shirt.

"Wait, my dear, you will know what engineers-to-be are up to," Motu replied while crushing the papers and placing them in a big deep cylindrical vessel.

They then put Maggi in a serving bowl with some water, set the bowl above the vessel and Anna lit the newspapers. While Vineet was holding the bowl, the others had to keep on adding newspapers to keep the fire lit.

Excellent teamwork had resulted in the water boiling. Our strategy had worked. We kept on adding newspapers to continue the fire and soon, a bowl of delicious Maggi was ready.

Though we had taken our own plates, we ate from the same bowl in which it had been cooked. We had two spoons for seven odd boys.

We took our seats around the bowl of Maggi, under the open sky. From our terrace, we could see the area of Russel Chowk and the main road which led to the station.

Rahul was a guitarist, and he was playing his guitar that night. The rhythm of the guitar was stupefying. Vineet asked me "*Kameene, sach batana*, are you flirting with Vaidehi or are you seriously in love with her?"

I looked at him, taking a spoonfull of Maggi and then replied, "So sitting in class together means I am flirting with her or do you want me to say we both love each other a lot and we are going to marry in a few days?" I asked him and smiled.

"Okay fine, I got it. Neither are you flirting with her, nor do you love her. Does she love you?" he asked me the second question.

I looked at him, "And what sort of question is that, Motu?"

"Does she love you? And if you will say no, my next question will be why did she follow you when Priti ma'am asked you to leave?" he questioned me acting like Dev Anand in the movie *CID*.

I smiled at him. "Well, the answers to these questions are with Vaidehi, so please go to her and clarify your doubts." Our silent terrace rang out with laughter.

I paused, putting another spoon of Maggi into my mouth and continued in a serious tone. "Motu, you've asked questions for which even I am searching the answers. I don't know why I sit with her. I don't know why her smile attracts me. I don't know what her eyes say. I don't know why she came along with me, but I know one thing, that I love Navya, and no smile or eyes can divert me from her love."

Everyone listened and then Anna said, "*Launda to senti ho gaya bhai.*" We all laughed heartily.

But Rahul left a perfect comment, "If you don't love her, don't make her feel loved. She'll end up getting hurt."

And then Rahul picked up his guitar and started playing the rhythm of the popular song from the movie *Pardes*.

"*Do dil mil rahe hain... magar chupke chupke... sab ko ho rahi hai... Khabar chupke chupke...*"

I sang along as he played. This continued till four in the morning. We sang many love songs, Anna and Vineet finished two packets of cigarettes, and the burned papers flew across the terrace before we made it back to our rooms.

Sunday mornings where lazy mornings in hostels. We were asleep till one in the afternoon when Chhotu, our hostel boy, came to my room, banging the door.

"Rohan *bhaiya, aapke ghar se phone aaya hai!*" he shouted from outside.

I could hear him screaming but could not open my eyes. He kept on banging. The afternoon sunlight had lit up my room by then. I opened my eyes rubbing them hard and tried to stand up, "Okay, I am coming!" I answered as I pulled out a t-shirt from the mess on my bed.

I ran down the quiet corridor. Almost everyone was asleep. By the time I reached the ground floor, the call had gotten disconnected. I gave a missed call, and Mom called me back.

"How are you, my *bacha*?" she said quietly. She was missing me a lot, I was sure.

"I am okay Mom, enjoying my college a lot. How are you all?"

"Everything is fine, except Surbhi," she replied.

"Why? What happened?" I asked worried.

"Nothing, she has chosen a boy named Anuj, and she wants to marry him only," she replied in a sad voice.

"So what is the problem? If she likes him, you must support her," I said pretending I knew nothing.

"You are correct, but Papa is a little worried. He is Brahmin. How would she adjust?"

"Mom, don't worry about her, she is a self-dependent girl and can always take care of herself. And so what if he is a Brahmin?" I explained to her.

She seemed convinced, but still sounded worried. The road was clear for Surbhi Di however, and I was thrilled.

After talking for a while longer, we said bye to each other and disconnected the call.

From the STD booth, I could see heavy traffic on the main road. Some of my seniors were standing outside chatting, looking at girls passing by. I was sweating inside that cabin and confused, thinking whether I should call Navya or not. I was looking at the red telephone, but my hands shivered. The STD booth owner was looking at me, wondering why I was sitting inside when the call was over. I smiled at him and so did he.

It had been a long time since I had last talked to her. Would she still remember me? Or would she refuse to speak with me?

Finally, I decided to go ahead and call her.

I picked up the receiver and started dialling her number, which I remembered by heart. But got confused and kept it back. I could feel the strain on both sides of my forehead.

Why was I so worried?

I redialled her number and waited as I could hear her phone ring.

"*Rohan, don't be scared, you are going to become an engineer now.*" I motivated myself.

Finally I heard her voice, "Hello?"

I could recognize her voice from thousands of voices, and hearing it felt like someone had poured cold water on me. "Hello," I said and I paused.

She also stopped speaking. Guess she was trying to place my voice. She finally replied, "Hello, Rohan?"

"Yes, you recognized me, thank god."

"Why praising god?" she asked.

"No, I called you after a long time, so was worried whether you'd recognize me or not."

She was quiet and I could hear her soft breath.

"How are you?" I continued.

"I am fine and what about you?"

"I thought this was the right time to call you. I am studying in an engineering college in Jabalpur now."

"Wow, congrats! I am so happy for you," she said.

And then there was a significant pause again. We had little to talk about, but then I asked her, "So what are you doing now?"

"Ah! I am pursuing my bachelor's in pharma from Sagar University."

"Great! That's an excellent institute."

Now it was the time when I must talk to her about our future and propose to her. I was however afraid of rejection and said, "Actually, I wanted to tell you something…"

"Ya, please tell me," she said.

"I… I was thinking… as you know… when we were in school…" Something was stopping me from saying '*I love you*' . I continued. "Well, just wanted to say… I miss school a lot."

She paused. "Yes, I know. But is this what you want to say to me?" she asked and I felt she was expecting something more from me, but my heart was stopping me from proposing to her.

"Yes, this is what I wanted to say to you."

"Okay then," she said.

"Keep in touch, bye," I replied and she responded before keeping her receiver down.

"You fool, Rohan. You are the biggest idiot," I scolded myself. She was waiting for you to propose and you missed the chance.

I sat in that cabin for a few more minutes, thinking if I was right, but I did not have any answers.

Did I like Vaidehi? But how come, we were still just friends? Why was I seeing Vaidehi's face when I was talking to Navya? Which one was infatuation and which was love? Vaidehi was steadily creeping on my mind, but I still loved Navya. Oh god, I was getting really confused between both.

My mind could not forget Vaidehi's attitude, her smile, her eyes and her gestures. Was I falling in love with her?

A proposal to visit Bhedaghat was being discussed in the class. It was located on the side of river Narmada and was twenty kilometres away from Jabalpur city. Its most famous sights are the Dhuandhar Falls, the Marble Rocks, and the Chaunsath Yogini temple.

Some of us took the responsibility of arranging bus, after getting everyone's consent.

I took a seat just behind Vaidehi, who was sitting with Chaaru.

It was a fun drive to Bhedaghat; we sang many songs and shared tiffins, finally reaching in the afternoon.

As we got down from the bus, which dropped us two kilometres from the main Dhuandhar Falls, Vaidehi held my hand and dragged me with her.

"Hey, what happened Vaidehi? *Kahan le ja rahi ho?*"

"Nowhere, can't you walk with me to the falls?" she replied stopping and looking at me.

I smiled and walked with her. She was enjoying herself a lot, smiling and looking at the shops full of marble knick knacks on both sides of the road. Soon after, she asked me, "You didn't answer the question I had asked you in the canteen that day."

"Which question?" I asked thinking back.

"Whether you love Navya or not?" she asked me again, stopping and looking deep into my eyes.

I moved forward, breaking eye contact with her. I could have said I loved her, but I didn't want to. She followed me and asked me the same question once more. I stopped, looked around and looked into her eyes, "What do you want to hear?"

"The truth," she replied.

I paused looking at her. "I love her or whether I loved her, I don't know the truth myself, and this is the truth."

"So you loved someone else?" her second question came.

"How does it matter?" I asked her.

She kept quiet and walked with me, and after a few minutes she asked another question. "Perhaps it matters, but I don't think it matters to you. So leave it. There's no point in discussing this."

I stopped waking and she stopped a few steps ahead of me, and turned back to look at me. "Sometimes you confuse me a lot, Vaidehi."

She smiled and asked me to walk along. After sometime, Chaaru along with two of our classmates, joined us.

"Hey Rohan, I am starving. Buy something for us, please," Chaaru asked me, making a face.

"Pull out your purse, and there is a shop you've crossed. Go back and buy some samosas for yourself," I replied teasing her.

"You are of no use Mr Rohan, carry on with this foolish Vaidehi," Chaaru said and left while Vaidehi smiled.

We kept on rambling silently now when Vaidehi spoke to herself pressing her stomach, "I am also starving now."

I heard it. I couldn't let that happen.

"You keep walking, I will be back shortly," I told her and ran back.

She watched me running for some seconds with her mouth open and then turned and walked towards Chaaru and the other girls.

I reached the spot where our bus was parked. I ran to a local tea shop there and got ten hot samosas packed.

I could not find her when I got back; perhaps she had reached the waterfalls. I hurried along and soon heard the sound of the waterfall.

In Bhedaghat, a major tourist attraction is the waterfall. It is known as Dhuandhar, as the gushing water looks like smoke coming out of the river – '*dhuan* (smoke) and *dhar* (flow of water)'.

I rushed towards it, crossing the railing under which the fast flowing waters of Narmada river flowed. I saw her taking a photograph of a view of the waterfall with Chaaru and the other girls. I rushed towards her, careful not to slip between the hard rocks.

As I reached her, she was facing the waterfall and talking to Chaaru. She didn't notice me. I kept both my hands on my waist and panted.

"Hey, Vaidehi!" I called her from behind

She turned and saw me wheezing. "What happened Rohan?"

I pulled myself up, still wheezing and forwarded the packet of samosas towards her.

"You were hungry, I heard."

She looked inside the package, smiled and then looked at me, "All these for me?"

I looked at her, showing my concern, "You were hungry, please eat all ten."

"Are you mad or what?" she said as Chaaru looked on.

Chaaru's eyes seemed to be saying "*When I asked, you replied so harshly and now you get ten samosas for Vaidehi... haan?*"

I saw her face and replied, "You can share a few with Chaaru too."

Vaidehi smiled as she picked up one samosa and passed the packet to the other girls.

Vaidehi then turned towards the railing next to the waterfall. I went and stood next to her.

She was quietly smiling, but there was a difference. She seemed to be pondering. I looked at her, and she spoke, without looking at me, "Ten samosas..." she giggled.

I also smiled, hearing her giggle.

"Can you imagine how high this fall is?" she asked me. I kept hearing her, and she spoke to herself, "Can someone love one's partner so much to be able to jump from this height for him or her?"

"I don't feel life must be given away for love. Turning your life in a direction which can make her happy is a greater way of loving her," I replied, mesmerized by the waterfall.

She took a bite from the samosa and offered it to me. I took it and placed it in her mouth, by opening her mouth with one hand and pushing the samosa with the other, laughing.

We enjoyed together, forgetting that there were others as well with us. When we returned to college in the evening, she took me aside and asked me, "You don't love her?"

I decided to keep quiet and smiled at her. I asked her if I could walk with her halfway to her home and she agreed. We both crossed the road when Vineet called me from behind and asked me to come along with him to a shop.

While I stood there with Vineet, she made her way home. I don't know why, but my heart kept telling me she wanted me to join her and that she would gesture me once more. I kept watching her as she continued walking alone.

It was nearly evening and weather had become cold by then. I kept watching her, thinking she'd turn towards me, but she kept walking, and after two minutes, she turned, stopped and gestured to me to join her.

"Vineet, you go ahead," I said to him and rushed toward Vaidehi, who was waiting for me at the corner.

"You are leaving your friend for a girl?" Vineet shouted, but I ignored him and ran towards her.

I stopped panting as I reached her, "Let's walk, I'll drop you home."

"Why did you come for me?" she asked me, with her head down. I looked at her. Her silver earrings sparkled. I looked at her and forgot Navya.

"Well, I couldn't let you walk all alone," I replied teasing her.

We crossed the fourth bridge and started walking towards Gorakhpur road. I saw that she was finding it difficult to carry her books in her hand. "May I carry your books?" I asked her chivalrously.

"No, it's okay," she replied. I walked and wondered why girls were so formal. If she were a boy, she would have given me all those books and the bag as well.

I stopped and took the books from her hands. She tried to stop me, but I didn't listen to her and walked on.

"As you wish, if you want to carry the load, you may," she taunted me and walked along, with a smile.

As we walked, she asked me something. "So, how did you propose to her?"

"Who?" I questioned her back

"You don't know who I am talking about?"

"Oh! About Navya?"

"So, do you have more girlfriends other than her?" she questioned me.

"Are you playing question-question with me?" I asked her laughing.

"Just reply to the question I asked you," she looked at my eyes and asked me straight.

I thought for a while. "I have not proposed to her, yet."

"What?" she stopped, in shock and continued speaking. "I cannot understand, she is your girlfriend, you love her but still you have not proposed to her. Then how can you say she loves you?"

I walked ahead without replying and she joined me expecting an answer. I could not understand what was going on. On the one hand, I was attracted to Vaidehi and I was confused about Navya. And now Vaidehi was making me more confused, by asking so many questions about Navya.

I told her, "It was teacher's day and the senior students of class eleventh and twelfth had thrown a party to all our teachers in school."

She listened intently. "As office-bearers, we were busy seeing to the arrangements and so we had our lunch after everyone else. I was serving lunch for myself when Navya came and asked if I could serve her some sweets. I helped her when one of my classmates came and interrupted us. 'Why don't you feed her with your spoon? Everyone knows what's going on between you two since the last one year,' he teased us.

"I tried to ignore him and asked Navya to ignore what he was saying. She smiled at me and moved to the other side of the hall and then turned back, looked at me and smiled again."

I was silent after narrating the story to her. We reached close to her house.

"Then, why didn't you propose to her; seems she loves you as well," she said, stopping on the side of the road.

"I don't know; something kept holding me back," I said slowly.

"You can never say the right thing at the right time!" she said. And pulling her books from my hands, she ran towards her house in a hurry. I kept standing looking at her; she closed her gate and waved goodbye.

What does she mean by that? What right thing? To whom? When?

What was she talking about? Navya or about herself? Why did I feel that she liked me? Did she want me to propose to her? But was I ready to propose to her? Or did I still love Navya?

I had no answers to the questions running in my heart and mind. My heart and soul seemed to have lost the sync with each other. They were working and performing actions without my permission. But I had no choice than to let them go free and take their decisions.

The first-semester exams were about to commence. Now it was time to get serious and focus on our studies. Engineers who studied throughout the session were not engineers; we studied just before the exams. During those days, the lights of the hostel remained switched on throughout the night. Students studying in groups were a common sight while a few remained alone on the terrace or locked in their rooms. The mess and recreation room remained deserted.

We refrained from going to college before the start of the exams so that we didn't waste a minute apart from the prep. I was extra cautious with my record of not being very good in my studies during school time. Vaidehi and Navya were out of sight and my mind. I was only concentrating on my studies.

The month of November had just started, and winter knocked on the doors of Jabalpur. Winters in Jabalpur were cold because of the marble around. I would have to go home in the semester break to collect my winter clothes from home. Also, we had planned to visit the Civic Centre to buy new sweaters the coming Sunday. Civic Centre in Jabalpur was famous for its trendy shops.

There was silence in the hostel that evening. The seniors' exams were over, and some of them had left for their homes and some were out having fun. Many had gone to watch a movie with their girlfriends. *Hum Sath Sath Hain* was on in the cinema halls. I was also waiting for my first paper to be over so that I could go to watch it. I had read that the movie was doing well, and Salman had a different look in it. But I had to wait for three more days.

We had our first test of Mathematics, and I was busy studying in my room that evening, along with Akash, who was studying on the bed. Akash was lying with a book in his hands. I preferred to study on my study table on which I had placed a small Lord Ganesha statue, not only to bless me but also to keep the table safe from dirty clothes and unwanted things. Chhotu suddenly came running to the room and informed me that a girl was waiting for me downstairs.

I was shocked to hear a girl had come to visit me in the hostel. Akash also looked at me in surprise. My relatives rarely came without informing me beforehand. Then who was it? Hope it was not a prank by a senior or Vineet, who loved doing such things. I stood up from my chair and grabbed my t-shirt hanging behind my chair.

I went out to the corridor and could hear Akash leaving our room and entering the room next to ours, while I went down the stairs.

One of my seniors coming up the steps looked at me and smiled, "Enjoy dear."

I was still not sure who was waiting outside and why my senior had spoken to me so. I hurried to the ground floor. The hostel attendant smiled at me. Some seniors were sitting on a sofa smoking. I greeted them and went outside. I was shocked to see Vaidehi sitting on her scooty, outside the hostel gate.

Most of my seniors where sitting in the lobby area and their eyes were on Vaidehi.

She should not have visited my hostel. Every other boy will talk about us now. No one will leave any stone unturned to tease me, I thought as I went up to her.

"Hi, how come you are here?" I asked her smiling.

"Can't I come to meet you?" she told me giving a big smile.

"No…. no.. Nothing like that but… it's a boy's hostel… you know," I replied.

She smiled further, holding the handle of the scooty with both her hands. She looked beautiful wearing short jeans and sea green top, with her hair open. Her pencil heels were making her look stunning. I had never seen her in such an outfit before.

I was worried about her being outside a boys' hostel.

She looked at me smiling and replied, "I know it's a boys' hostel. It's evident from the top window of the first floor."

Hearing her, I looked over and saw ten of my friends peeping at her from one window, including Akash, Vineet, and Anna.

But she looked cool and ignored them. "I am sorry for my friends' behaviour," I said with my head down.

"Nothing to worry about. But why are they watching us like this?" she asked me.

"Well, I guess we know why they are looking at you," I replied in a soft tone.

She became a little conscious hearing me, "Okay, so, can you handover your engineering drawing sheet for our project work? I need to copy it."

"Okay fine. Give me two minutes," I replied and turned back to the window and shouted to Akash who was also peeping. "Hey Akash, can you bring my engineering drawing project sheet down please, she needs it."

I shouted so that everyone could hear that she was there for work and not just to see me.

Akash got conscious, "Ya… ya I am bringing it!"

I asked her about her preparation. She was worried because revision was pending while here I was happy to complete my syllabus for the first time before the exam.

I could see some of my seniors signalling me from another side, out of her sight, to kiss her, hug her, and so on. I didn't look at them.

Soon Akash came running, with the engineering drawing sheet in his hand "Hey Vaidehi, how are you? Your sheet."

"Thanks Akash" she replied and continued. "What were you looking at from that window?" she asked him taunting.

Akash didn't know what to say, and then he murmured. "Nothing, I was waiting for Rohan to tell me... if he..." he stammered.

She smiled at his answer, took that sheet and kept it in the boot space of the scooty. She thanked me and smiled, "All the best," she said. She started her scooty and went off, saying bye.

I stood watching her when she stopped her scooty again. I took long steps and reached back her and asked,

"What happened?"

She looked at me and replied, "You look handsome with a beard," referring to the stubble that was the result of the focus on my studies.

She raised the accelerator and moved fast, without turning back. I smiled and watched her till she turned the corner. I looked around to see my seniors running towards me.

They all teased me, and I took it all in good fun. Someone so pretty visiting me had turned me into the hero of the hostel. My seniors began to address me as Vaidehi instead of Rohan. I became so comfortable that I even answered them when they call me Vaidehi. Sometimes I felt that I rather loved to be called by her name.

Everything around me changed with her name. People in the hostel had assumed that she was my girlfriend.

I was realizing now, how far Navya was left behind and how close Vaidehi was to me. I felt she was more beautiful than the winter sun above the Jabalpur marble rocks; she was warmer than spring sunshine on soft new grass; she was more mesmerizing than the fall leaves. For me, she truly was eternal summer, for every day with her looked perfect with blue skies and love in the air. My attraction to her wasn't just because she was gorgeous, it was to the wonderful person she was inside.

Exams were over, and I was excited to go home for fifteen days. Most of us were packing our bags in the hostel that day, shouting and singing. It was seven in the evening and dark by then. I packed up my bag and hugged Akash, who would leave the next day.

Thakur was waiting to drop me to Damoh Naka from where I'd catch my bus. I moved to every room on my floor and hugged my friends and wished them happy holidays. Everyone was instructed to bring the best food from their cities when they returned.

I walked downstairs where Thakur was waiting for me on his scooter. I waved goodbye to my friends and seniors on the ground floor and stepped out. Thakur smiled at me asking me to sit quickly as he needed to leave for his uncle's home after dropping me. I was singing loudly in excitement, while Thakur looked sad as he said he would feel lonely in these fifteen days.

It was cold by then. I folded my hands hiding behind Thakur to save myself from the cold wind. Thakur rode fast, crossing heavy traffic, and promptly took me to Damoh Naka from where I would get my bus.

Damoh Naka was over-crowded. People carrying bags on their shoulders and heads were searching for buses. Multiple buses coming in and moving out was adding to the hustle and bustle. I thanked Thakur for dropping me and asked him to leave. I also asked him to let me know when the results were out; I had given him my roll number.

"*Chal, milte hain soon,* bye take care," he told me, hugged and left. I pulled up my bag again on my back; it was heavy as I was carrying all my dirty clothes and some gifts for Papa, Mummy and Surbhi Di. I looked around and saw a white bus standing on the side of the road with 'Sahani Travels' written on it and a board on its windscreen that said 'Sagar'. I understood that was the private travel bus which would leave for Sagar in sometime.

I stepped into the bus and took my seat. Leaning against the windowpane, I fell asleep.

I reached my hometown at six in the morning. The bus conductor shouted that the bus had reached its destination. I opened my eyes from deep sleep. Rubbed my eyes and looked out of the window. It was foggy outside.

I stepped down and looked around. The bus stand was empty. The sky was getting brighter with every passing minute. The chirping of birds started on the peepul tree next to the tea stall. I pulled up the zip of my jacket as it was cold.

I walked to my house which was close by. I looked at the familiar places and spots, which I had missed during the last few months. I remembered Vaidehi and smiled thinking about her and her gestures.

I was planning to meet Navya but was confused, as my mind was getting more inclined towards Vaidehi. Should I meet Navya and propose to her or should I propose to Vaidehi? Sometimes I felt I loved both equally. But that would not lead anywhere. I had to take a decision.

By the time I reached home, it was bright. The shops outside my house were closed, and children were waiting for the school bus to come. Time flies so fast. It seems like a few days back I was also a school going child, boarding the same bus with my friends and cousins.

I reached home and rang the bell. No one knew that I was coming and this would be a surprise for them. The door opened, and I saw Papa, trying to figure out from inside who was there. Surprised, he welcomed me opening the door. I touched his feet and hugged him.

"You surprised us!" he hugged me while Mom came out hearing my voice and hugged me too.

I moved to my room and saw Surbhi Di still sleeping. I pressed her cheeks, and she woke up in surprise seeing me. She hugged me saying, "Missed you, Bhai."

"So how is Anuj?" I asked teasing her.

My mom was happy to see me and had already planned what she would cook for me. I had lost a lot of weight, and she wasn't happy about it.

Surbhi Di stood up from the bed and pulled me to my study room, holding my hand. She was in a hurry to show me something.

"Where are you dragging me, Didi?" I asked.

"Got something to show you, close your eyes."

I did as she said, but could feel I was moving to my study room. She switched on the light and asked me to open my eyes.

As I opened my eyes, I saw the picture of Navya and me in school framed and placed on the wall. I looked at it in surprise and then looked at my sister, who was waiting to see my smile. I don't know why, but I could only give a fake smile.

"Who put it here?" I asked looking at her.

"Well, I asked Mom to put it here as you love her a lot," she replied and continued, "You helped me convince Mom about Anuj, *itna to banta tha.*"

I turned back and took a seat on my bed, still looking at the framed picture hanging on my room wall.

"You don't like it?" she asked me.

"No... no, it's not like that. It's great, thanks," I replied faking some excitement.

I liked that picture, and what else I could expect as a gift that my parents had accepted Navya. But what about Vaidehi? What if her picture had been hanging here with me?

Surbhi Di left me alone in my room, and I kept looking at the picture, puzzled about what I must do. Should I meet her and let her know what I feel about her? Or just forget about her?

I had a bath and then breakfast with my family and attended a few calls from my old school friends, who were also back for the holidays. I called Vikram's house and was told he would come the next day.

It was a bright sunny day and what can be better than the sun in winter. I went to the terrace and was enjoying the sunlight when Surbhi Di turned up. Papa had planted a lot of flowers on the terrace and there was a riot of colours.

She found me confused, but she wanted to understand the reason behind it. She asked me if I was seeing someone else now and had lost interest in Navya. I heard her and then looking at the mango trees far away, I said, "Don't know what happened. I still love her a lot, but maybe I love someone more. She is in my batch. Her name is Vaidehi. She is my best friend whereas everyone in college thinks she is my girlfriend. And I am still confused about our relation. When I am with her, I remember nothing and want to be with her only, and when I am away from her, Navya takes over my mind. And when I believe that I love Navya, Vaidehi takes over her again. I am too confused, di."

She listened to me carefully and then replied, "There is no confusion brother. You love Vaidehi." I looked at her to understand how she could she be so sure. And then she explained, "Since the last two years, no other girl distracted you from Navya. Nothing could keep you away from her. But Vaidehi did that in seconds. Obviously, she has that magic in her. Believe me, you love Vaidehi."

I heard her carefully and realized she was right. I wasn't confused any longer. I pressed her cheeks again, and screamed, "Thanks, sis! I love you a lot."

"So shall I propose to her?" I asked her seriously.

"Immediately, before someone else does," she concluded. "Brother, sometimes in love you don't need to think...let it go. Just close your eyes for a minute and check who among the two of them you see most of the time."

I heard her and did as she told. I closed my eyes for a minute and could only find Vaidehi smiling at me. I could feel her near me; I could feel her smile. She was nowhere near me, but it felt as if she was everywhere near me. I was now sure I loved Vaidehi.

I decided to propose to her on New year's eve, as it would be a good day to start the year with love. I would return to Jabalpur on 2nd January, so could meet her the next day for a big hug.

Spending each day was tough, every day I was rehearsing the proposal for hours in front of the mirror. My mom was worried wondering why I spent so much time in the washroom or locked in my room. She often said to Papa, "*Mera beta badal gaya hai, akela sa rehta hai.*"

It was new year's eve, and I was all set to propose to her. I informed my sister that I would go to the nearby STD booth to have a word with Vaidehi. She gave me her best wishes.

As I made my way on my papa's scooter, I could see fireworks already, their light spreading in the sky. It was freezing that day. I wore the jacket I had bought from the Civic Centre. The roads were crowded and people were in a mood to celebrate. I parked my scooter outside the STD booth and went inside. It was quite a rush there. I selected a booth that had a sound proof calling room.

I took a seat and picked up the receiver. My heart was beating fast, ears became hot and I felt a pain on both sides of my head. I was too nervous. What will happen if she rejects me? What if I lose her friendship? Such questions were taking over my mind.

I noticed a line on a poster placed inside. *'Talk relevant; other are waiting.'*

I must talk clearly to her; many more boys were waiting for her. I was sure I loved her and remembered our bond. I was sure she loved me too.

I dialled her number. I was sweating in the month of January. I could hear the ringtone and then someone picked up the phone. It was her brother.

"May I speak to Vaidehi?" I asked. Hearing me, he asked my name. He kept the phone on hold and shouted her name. I could listen to the sound of steps running fast to the phone. She picked up the receiver, "Hello, who's this?"

"It's me, Rohan," I managed to say.

"Are you back or calling me from Sagar?" she asked.

"No, still in Sagar, will be back tomorrow."

"Ya, so tell me, what's happening Mr Verma?" she asked.

"Happy new year to you and your family," I began. She greeted me too. After she had completed, I continued, "I want to tell you something else."

"What happened, is everything okay?" she asked

I was really scared now. I could feel the sweat on my forehead. My eyes stopped blinking, and I could hear nothing except my heartbeat. "I love you!" I finally let it out.

I paused, and she was silent, "I said I love you. Whenever I am with you, I keep looking at you, and when I am not with you, I still keep dreaming of you. I see you smiling when I close my eyes and dream about you with my open eyes. When you are near, I want to touch you; when you touch me, I want to hug you. You've changed me entirely. I am no longer Rohan Verma and want to become Rohan Sharma for you," I concluded.

She heard it quietly and then replied "Oookay."

I was afraid that she would give me a tight slap on the phone itself and was afraid to hear her say no. I decided to keep the phone down. "Okay bye. I said what I wanted to say, bye," I spoke in a hurry and decided to keep down the receiver, but she broke her silence. "Rohan, please stop, do not keep the phone down. Talk to me."

"No, I am not in a position to talk to you now," I replied

"Listen, Rohan, we are great friends, talk to me," she spoke loudly to stop me from keeping the phone back.

I held on, "Yes, tell me."

"See, why are you speaking like this? I am fine about what you said to me. We can discuss this when you will come back to college day after tomorrow. So, relax Rohan," she said making me comfortable.

"Thanks for understanding. Okay then, we will meet in college," I said and disconnected the call.

After keeping the receiver back, I leaned back on the wall. I was still sweating, but feeling relaxed after speaking out my heart. Hope I had expressed nothing wrong. She hadn't replied, nor had she scolded me. It could be because she loved me too. I began smiling. After paying the bill, I hurried home. I wanted to reach home and discuss it with my sister. This was the first time in many years that I was not missing Navya at all.

While I was driving, my mind was recalling each word I had said. My mind was out of control. I never had such a feeling that I had that day. It's so tough to propose to a girl whom you love as there's always the fear of rejection.

When I reached home, it was dark. Surbhi Di was with mom, who was frying *pooris* and she was helping her. Papa was sitting on the dining table. Surbhi Di looked at me and raised her eyebrows questioningly. I gestured to her, hiding from Papa.

Papa was listening to BBC news on his radio, which he loved a lot. Everyone was quiet and busy listening to the news. I stood up and disturbing no one went towards my room. Soon, Didi also followed me, giving some excuse.

I laid down on my bed, with eyes wide open, with Vaidehi's face in front of me, smiling at me. Surbhi Di entered the room and asked "What happened Rohan? What did she say?"

I looked at her, smiled, "She didn't say yes, but she also did not say no."

"Tell me in detail," she asked me.

I stood up and closed the door of my room and told her everything that had happened. She heard me with patience, and as I completed, she looked at me smiling, "So, she said yes. I am so happy for you Rohan."

"But she never said yes, she asked me to meet her in college."

"Oh my sweet little brother, I understand girls better than you. Girls are clear in their thoughts. If she had not liked you, she would have said no straightaway. She continued talking to you even after you proposed to her. That is a sign that she loves you. So, relax and throw me a party," she said like an experienced teacher. I was too happy to hear her words. I understood that Navya was not my true love and so I could never propose to her.

I was now more concerned about my future with her and changes this proposal would bring in my college life. I was happy to have found someone with whom I would spend my whole future. Let god give me the strength to keep her smiling throughout her life and make me her reason to smile.

I was thrilled to go to college and was excited, yet afraid to meet her.

"Are you okay? Looking tense," Akash said while we were getting ready for the first day of our second semester. I smiled at him and assured him that everything was fine. But he calmly looked at me as he had observed changes in me.

"No, you are not all right. You have sprayed almost half a bottle of deodorant, you have been setting your hair since the last ten minutes, and also you've used mouth freshener. You never used to do these things before," he observed. And he wasn't wrong. My proposal to Vaidehi made me extra conscious about myself. I was more aware presently that someone was there who would be more interested in me than engineering classes.

I turned to him, smiled and sat back on the bed with my hands on my back and continued laughing.

"Something happened? Tell me, *kameene?*" he yelled and sat next to me.

"I proposed to her," I replied with a shy smile on my face. I think I was blushing. He stood up in shock.

"What? You proposed to whom?"

I looked at him with a pleasant expression on my face. "Yes, I proposed Vaidehi."

His face was blank, with wide eyes open in front of me. "Oh Bhai, what was her response? She must have agreed."

"Not exactly, but again, she did not say no to my proposal. She wants to take a final decision after college, meantime she intends to continue as a friend," I said.

"Beta, if she has not rejected you, that means she has accepted. Too happy for you and bhabhi," he said and danced in excitement.

Bhabhi! He had called her 'bhabhi'. I was yet not sure how to face her, and here he had called her bhabhi.

"She will kill me if she hears you calling her bhabhi. Control your excitement and let's go to college. And remember, don't show your emotions in front of her," I asked him to hide his excitement in front of everyone in college.

As we approached college, our civil engineering class had already begun. We were late. I reached the class entrance and asked permission to enter. Vaidehi was sitting in the front seat and looked at me smiling. I avoided eye contact with her, moved in and sat right behind her, although the seat next to her was vacant.

As I took a seat, she turned back and smiled looking at me, expecting a reply. But I was extremely nervous to face her. I looked down at my books.

Her smile was making me somewhat nervous. I could not face the one person I was deeply in love with. During the class, she tried talking one more time by asking me for a pen which I handed over to her, without looking at her eyes. She looked at me making a face, pulling the pen from my hands.

As the class got over, I stood up and left before she could even talk to me. Why was I doing that? I don't know. I avoided her at lunch time too and went to the canteen with Anurag and Vineet. I could see she was very annoyed with my behaviour.

Later in the day, half of our batch was in the civil practical lab, where our teacher was explaining to us various stress levels, while the remaining half was attending the field practical about dumpy level. I attended the lab class whereas she was in the field practical. We always choose field practical as we can enjoy chatting, but that day I avoided it.

"Did you both fight?" Chaaru asked me quietly in the middle of the class.

"No, not at all" I replied and tried concentrating on the session, even though my mind was roaming with her in the field practical.

Sir was busy explaining to us various stress levels on the blackboard when someone knocked at the door. It was Vaidehi.

"Yes, what happened?" Sir asked her making a face, as she had disturbed him in middle of the class.

"Sir, our practical field class is over," she replied with her hands behind her back.

"So, you want to join this session?"

"No sir, I want to ask if Rohan can get excused from your class." I was shocked. The others smiled at me while the professor stared at her unblinking.

"And may I know why should I excuse him?" he asked making a strange face.

"Sir, he has not had lunch today and even I haven't. I request you to excuse him so that we can have our lunch," she explained confidently to him, while I gestured her to leave, but she was adamant.

Sir got angry and asked her to leave. She asked him again, but he only asked her to leave. She turned around with a sad face, looking down. I quickly stood up and walked towards her.

"Can you please sit down? I have not permitted you to leave!" Sir shouted at me.

"Sir, I am really hungry. Since the last two days, I have not had the food in the hostel. My intestines are drying up. I may die if I don't eat, please excuse me," I said while I ran towards her. From my class, I saw her at a distance. I know our Civil teacher was very angry with me, but she was more important.

"So, can we have lunch?" I touched her shoulder from behind and spoke to stop her. She turned and laughed looking at me. I was expecting a hug from her.

"You jerk!" She said and held my hand and dragged me to a corner behind the trees, behind the classrooms. This was a corner where we used to hide when we bunked classes. She came closer and I could feel her breath. First time after I proposed to her, I looked deep into her beautiful eyes.

"Why have you been avoiding me since morning?" she asked looking into my eyes while I looked down.

"Look into my eyes" she insisted. I did and said, "I don't know why I am avoiding you."

After a pause, I continued, "It seems you are my girlfriend."

She smiled, while I kept looking at her and then said, "You proposed to me, then why are you afraid now?"

"I am not afraid," I tried saying confidently, but my voice shivered. Her lips were glossy and were asking me to kiss her, but my fear had overtaken my desire.

"Then why are you running away from me?" she asked coming even closer. Her kurti was touching my shirt now, and I was feeling shy.

"I can't only be your friend and wait for your answer till the last day of college. I can't sit with you without holding your hands, can't stop myself from considering your beautiful eyes, can't keep my hands from disentangling your hair. Every time I look at your smiling lips, I wonder what's holding me back from kissing you." and I halted, as I felt her glossy pink lips over my lips. Yes, she had kissed me. Her lips tasted great. Time stopped, sensations went still, and after a few seconds, she moved her lips from mine, stepped back continuing eye contact and pulled out her tiffin box and put it in my hand. "You can eat this tiffin," she said and smiled at me, leaving me stunned as she left.

What had happened was unbelievable. I kept standing there for fifteen minutes, trying to understand what had happened between us. I had got the best reply to my proposal.

Next day, precisely after twenty hours, nine minutes and thirty-six seconds, Vaidehi was sitting in front of me in our classroom, which was empty as class had not yet started.

"Stop thinking and let's talk," she interrupted my thoughts with her melodious voice.

I nodded, looking at her, "Forget what happened yesterday, we are here to study and secure our future," she added.

"Future in?" questioned innocently.

"I know where you are up to Mr Rohan. I am serious now," she replied hitting me on my shoulder with a book she was holding.

"Remember, we both will remain like friends as others in college, no one will ever know we are together," she explained the conditions and continued. "No touching further, and we will concentrate on our studies."

While she was explaining, her feet touched me, and she immediately brought her hand to me. I looked at it and then back to her eyes.

"What? C'mon, I am a devi na, touch my hand and say sorry," she told me.

"I can't; you said no touching," I replied innocently.

She pulled her hands back and said softly, "Touching my hand is allowed."

I listened to her, smiled and held her hand. "I said touching is allowed, not holding," she said smiling.

I kept holding her hand "So, no kissing for the next three years?" I asked her, making an innocent face.

She pulled back her hand, "Mr Rohan, stop dreaming. Nothing like that will happen again."

I stood up, moved to the door and then peeped outside; no one was there in the corridor. I went back to her and stood behind her. She was sitting on a chair, opening a book. I leaned over her and kissed on her cheeks from the back.

She stood up in shock and slapped me on my shoulder. "Rohan, I told you no touching, and you kissed me again!" she shouted at me smiling.

"You kissed me yesterday. I was just returning it," I said.

She was now standing in front of me with a book in her right hand and her left hand on her waist. She had a mischievous smile on her face.

"Where is my interest of twenty hours, twenty minutes and forty seconds?" she said and put her lips on my lips and we kissed again.

She pulled herself back, collected her books and went to the classroom door. She stopped at the entrance, turned and replied, "Remember, if you speak about this to any of your friends or if anyone comes to know that we are a couple, I will stop talking to you."

I touched my lips with my thumb. What a moment it was. I smiled at her and sat on the chair with my legs on the desk.

When she had kissed me, I felt as though my brain was on fire, and the warmth spread throughout my body. After that, I was addicted. I couldn't bear not to be with her, and I could barely breathe when she was around. Those kisses were my salvation and my torment. I lived for them, and I would die with the memory of them on my lips. I dedicated my life to be with her from the moment of that first kiss, for I knew that if I lost her, I would lose myself. She was the half that made me whole.

My love life bloomed with every passing day. I could feel her presence in every thought of my life. Her smile, her attitude, her lips, her moves – everything was precious for me and being with her was a dream which I was living.

The second semester was my best semester. Except for my hostel friends, I had only one friend in my life, and she was Vaidehi. Every morning, I picked her up and we went to college together. During class, we always sat together. She regularly carried another tiffin for me, and we'd spend time in the library or an empty classroom. It was evident to everyone that we were a couple, no matter how hard we tried to hide the fact.

It was midnight; we walked to Fauji Dhaba, which was a dhaba near the Jabalpur railway station. The Fauji Dhaba opened at 8:30 in the evening and closed at five in the morning. It was our favourite night food joint. Except for the start of the month, we never had money in our pockets. So Fauji Dhaba always took the first position in our hearts.

That night, I went to Fauji Dhaba along with Vineet, Anna, Akash, Rahul, Raman, Majhar and a few other guys. We were hungry as usual. I was wearing my boxers and a white t-shirt gifted by Vaidehi on Valentine's Day. Her gift was close to my heart, and I wore it at night to feel her presence.

We stepped out of the hostel and informed Chhotu to open the gate when we return and not to let the warden know about this.

"Your t-shirt is cute. Where did you buy it?" Vineet asked me while we were walking. I didn't want to tell him, that it was a gift from Vaidehi. "From where did you buy it?" he persisted.

But this time, Akash replied with a cruel, teasing smile, "It's a Valentine's Day gift."

I quickly interrupted him. "Nothing like that, my mom gave it to me."

Vineet took a long step and came in front of me. He peeped to check my t-shirt.

"'Love you *Janu*.' Your mom gifted you a t-shirt with such a slogan?" he asked me stopping.

"So what, Mom can't call me janu?" I tried to defend myself.

Akash gave a wicked smile, hiding his face. I slapped him in fun, "Stop laughing, you rascal."

Vineet was observing me, and replied, "Okay, if it's gifted to you by your mom, let's exchange our t-shirts."

"Now how can I take my t-shirt off on the road?" I replied with an attitude.

"Why, you are not a boy? We walked naked while ragging. Please take your t-shirt off. I want it, I love it," he insisted.

"Haan, haan Rohan, give your t-shirt to Vineet," Akash joined in.

Vineet had pulled off his t-shirt and was waiting for me to give him my t-shirt. I was in trouble now; either I had to give my t-shirt to him or I had to confess. I ran towards Fauji Dhaba instead. Vineet and Akash followed to catch me and so did my other friends. I had hardly run fifty metres, when they grabbed me and started pulling off my t-shirt.

I shouted, "Motu, guys, hold on! I can't give you my t-shirt."

"Then confess Rohan," they yelled.

I hesitated but needed to confess to save my t-shirt. "It's a gift from Vaidehi, understand friends."

They soon left me. Vineet was laughing out loud along with Akash. "We all knew it's from Vaidehi, but wanted to hear it from your mouth. We are your friends, and we have a right to know about our 'bhabhijaan'."

"Okay okay. I confess, she is my girlfriend, and she gifted me this t-shirt."

Hearing this, they shouted loudly on the road, taking her name aloud.

"Congrats!"

"We have a Bhabhi now!"

"Rohan *ki* Vaidehi!"

I was happy to have friends like them, who were so happy and concerned for me. That night, I was the party boy, and paid the bill for everyone at Fauji Dhaba.

We returned at two and went into our rooms. Vineet came to our room, along with Akash. We turned off the lights and chatted. There was light coming in from the lamp post just outside our room.

Vineet opened a window as he was smoking.

"Why you were hiding this from us?" Vineet asked me while taking a long puff.

I thought for a while and replied, lying on his lap. "She is not comfortable, as of now."

"And what about your school girlfriend, what was her name, Navya?"

"I think it was an infatuation. I don't dream about her anymore," I replied placing my hand on my t-shirt.

"So when are you introducing us to her, again, like bhabi this time?" he asked me.

I smiled listening to him, but I couldn't take him to her. "Not now bhai. I don't want her to get conscious about our relationship, understand brother."

Being a good friend, he understood my concern and agreed.

My love life was running perfectly. My mind and heart were singing love songs.

I used to sing a lot of songs for her, and she cherished them a lot. We were together the whole day now, along with Chaaru, who consistently felt like a '*kabab mein haddi*'.

Chaaru often commented to Vaidehi that she was growing fairer in my love, and we always laughed at her strange observation.

Our first semester results were out. Anurag came rushing to my hostel that morning. I was still lazying on my bed listening to songs on my Walkman while Akash was wasting water in the washroom.

"Buddy, results are out! Get ready, let's go to college," Anurag shouted, banging on my door. Listening to him, some others gathered in my room as well. Everyone was nervous and excited.

"*Mera to pakka he ruk gaya hoga ek subject,*" Anna spoke in fear.

Anurag was a local and such information reached to him on the phone. He was sure about the results, and he came to the hostel first so he could take me along. I banged on the washroom door and asked Akash to come out fast. Soon, we were ready for college.

My heart beat harder; the shadow of my school results was behind me. Would I pass or not? As we entered the college gate, we could see a huge mob in front of the notice board, shouting and trying to check their results.

We stepped down from the scooter and rushed towards it. Vikram congratulated me as Vaidehi has topped. Wow, I was so happy for her. She deserved it. She was not only perfect in looks, but excellent in studies too.

I looked around, but could not find her nearby. I rushed towards the notice board to check up my result. I tried to move in with the mob while Anurag pushed everyone to create some space.

We started searching for our results. I had managed to pass all the subjects with seventy-three percent.

I then checked the percentage of Vaidehi's results. Eighty-nine. She had topped the college. 'I love you,' I whispered.

I managed to get out of the crowd and joined Anurag, who was sitting on the stairs next to the notice board.

"Hey Thakur, what happened? What' s your result?"

He looked like he was going to burst into tears. "Failed in one subject."

I tried to console him, "No worries yaar, don't take it seriously. It's only one subject; you will clear that in the compartment scheduled."

While I was consoling him, Akash came with a sad face along with Vineet, who was laughing.

"What happened Vineet, your result?"

"*Hona kaya hai,* I failed in all five subjects and Akash in two," he again laughed.

"F**k man and you are laughing?" said Anurag who was in a serious mood.

"Listen, I may have failed, but will become an engineer one day," Vineet replied laughing.

While we were engrossed in the discussions, I saw Vaidehi on the other side of the building. I could see her from the open space of the window. I rushed towards her.

"Hey, Vaidehi!" I shouted from a distance as she almost moved on her scooty. Hearing my voice, she stopped and turned to me with a smile. Chaaru stepped down, who was sitting at the back seat.

"Congrats!" I told her with a light hug, holding my breath.

"You know, there's an annual function in our campus next month," she said, while I was expecting her to ask my results.

"Really? You don't want to know my results?" I asked her, making a face

"Checked your results before I checked mine, and am happy for you. But am more excited about the annual function," she replied and continued. "We will take part in the dance, what say?"

"Sure, would love to dance with you. Ball dance?" I replied being naughty.

"Shut up, group dance on old song – *Aaj kal tere mere pyaar ke charche har zubaan par,*"she confirmed.

"And who told you all these details?"

"I met Anjum Sir; he said that our batch would perform on this song."

She came closer and then asked softly in a real serious voice, "Hope we are not famous in college as a couple as of now."

The wind blew her hair on her face. I blinked my eyes in worry and replied "No, we are still best buddies. No one knows we are a couple."

She paused and then questioned me, "Then why are some of your hostel friends laughing at us from behind?"

As I heard her, I immediately turned and saw Majhar, Vineet, Anna making naughty faces, looking at us and laughing. I shouted at them, "What happened?"

They understood. "Nothing Rohan, carry on." They laughed again and moved to another side.

This incident made her conscious, and her face changed. She again asked me, "Rohan, I trust you. Hope they don't know about us?"

I gestured to her, confirming about it and then questioned, "What if they know? Are we not a couple?"

She looked tense removing the strands of hair from her face. "We are a couple, but I am from a conservative family. My father knows many faculty members, and if he comes to know about this, there will be big trouble."

"But one day he will get to know," I replied.

"I know, but that day you will be well established, and I will have reason to convince him," she tried to explain to me.

I looked into her eyes and said, "I assure you, I love you and no one will ever come to know that we are a couple."

She again smiled, and so did I, but I was worried as I was telling a lie to her. Almost everyone in the hostel knew about our affair. My friends knew that I love her, and my friends knew I had kissed her. I knew I had made a mistake by telling my close friends, but even if I had not told them, it was evident we were together. What would she do if she came to know that I had lied to her? But I was sure about my love, and that I would convince her under any circumstances.

The next day, the audition for the dance started.

Anjum Sir was standing on the stage in the auditorium with a few students gathered around him. He was explaining the theme of the dance our batch was about to perform. We both went and stood with the others. He explained that this dance would have pairs – one boy, and one girl. It was a song from an old Bollywood movie and the pairs needed to gel well.

Vaidehi and I were excited on hearing this; it would be great to dance as a pair. I touched her hand and expressed my excitement.

Once Anjum Sir completed his briefing, he asked all the interested candidates to give their names in pairs. I immediately rushed to him and asked him to enroll both of us.

Anjum Sir looked at us and replied, "You both cannot be partners. Please choose different partners," he said bluntly which was unexpected.

"But sir, why? We want to dance as partners," I insisted while Vaidehi listened to him with a serious face.

"At least let her be for the performance, Rohan," he told me laughing. He continued, "In this performance, you will not suit together. Try out different partners."

I could not say anything further and turned to Vaidehi. She was standing looking angry. She looked at me and moved out of the auditorium. I rushed to her, calling her name. She stopped outside the auditorium, hiding behind a pillar.

I reached her and saw she had tears in her eyes. "Hey Vaidehi stop crying dear, he thinks we do not match for this performance. Don't be disheartened; it's only his view."

But she would not stop. She pulled out her handkerchief and wept.

"Please stop, I love you. Doesn't matter if we can't dance together. We are always together baby," I tried to console her.

She looked at me. I wanted to hold her. And then she replied, "I am not concerned about the dance, Rohan. Why did he say 'at least let her be for this performance.' Isn't it evident he knows we are together?"

I knew she loved me, but her concern that no one must come to know was puzzling me a lot.

"Why you are so concerned about this? You love me, and I love you. Damn the others. I am not afraid of anyone," I said aggressively.

"But it matters a lot to me Rohan," she answered in a loud voice, wiping her tears.

"You tell me then, how can I stop them. We are together, and it's the truth. One day it will be known to everyone. How can we hide it?" I tried to reason.

She turned her face away from me and looked at the other side. I stood behind her and waited for her response. She walked to the other side without looking at me and went to Akash who was standing with one of our classmates.

"Akash, will you be my partner in the dance for the annual function?" she asked him tapping on his shoulder.

Akash turned to her and then looked at me. I didn't want her to cry further. I gestured to Akash to say yes.

"Oh sure, why not. Even I was looking for a partner," he replied smiling.

I stood behind her silently, with my hands on my waist, broken and hurt. She thanked Akash and informed him she was giving his name as her partner to Anjum Sir.

"Are you sure Vaidehi?" I asked holding her hand as she crossed me.

"It's a must Rohan. We need to show people that we are not a couple, and this would help us," she replied and was clear in her thought.

I heard her, but asked her one last question, "Are you sure? Everyone knows we are a couple."

She replied, "I am cautious and this is what I feel is right."

Maybe she was correct. I might see a picture from my angle, but she would look at it from a different perspective.

The same evening, I was still disturbed by what had happened in college. I looked at the watch and saw that it was time for dinner. I locked the room and went to the mess. My steps were slow that day; I was feeling dull and depressed.

I was worried about Vaidehi's concern. She didn't want our relationship to be public, but the situation was beyond my control.

As I reached the mess, I saw Akash, Vineet, Anna and a few more friends, along with a few seniors having dinner. There were three long tables joined to make a big table for dinner and benches were placed on both sides.

"Oye Vaidehi, welcome to the mess of rock stars," Vineet welcomed me as the others laughed aloud. I tried to ignore them and took my plate. Teasing is one of the favourite activities in the hostel and everyone loved it, without considering that they might hurt someone.

There was rajma, rice and chapattis for dinner that night. I served myself while Akash commented, "What happened Rohan? I think she is more interested in me, no!"

And once more, everyone laughed. I tried to ignore him, took my food and sat next to Rahul.

"What happened? Looking dull, had a fight with her or what?" Akash again questioned with a smile on his face.

I faked a smile but something was hurting me. I ate my dinner quietly while they chattered. Rahul was having his dinner silently when I questioned him quietly, "Why were you all laughing at us in college today?"

Hearing my voice, the others stopped talking and looked at me, "Is it wrong to smile at our Bhabhi?" Vineet replied taunting.

"I told you all never to reveal that you all know about my relationship in front of her."

"*Aaj bhabhi ne kiss nahi kiya shayad,*" Anna responded to tease me further, but I was not in a good mood that evening. I threw my plate in the air in anger and caught hold of Anna's shirt and shouted.

"You fool, don't take my friendship for granted. I will not leave you if you mess with my relationship."

My eyes went red; muscles tight.

Anna pushed me hard, and I fell from the bench. The others also stood up and tried to restrain me. The seniors who were sitting there also shouted at me to stop, but I was full of anger and picked up a plate which was lying in front of me and threw it at them. I struck Anna on his back while Vineet and Akash tried to stop me. I went mad and hit them. Finally, Vineet punched me on my face, and I fell.

I was bleeding from my nose. I shuffled aside and pressed my nose to stop the bleeding. Vineet and the others stood looking at me while the seniors kicked us apart and scolded us. Rahul pulled out some cotton from a medical box kept in the mess and cleaned my nose. I removed his hand and kept looking at them for a while and then cried loudly while shouting, "You all don't love me, guys. Shame on you! You made me uncomfortable in front of the one I love the most in my life. Because of you, I made her cry... aaaahhh!" I yelled much louder.

Rahul was still trying to hold my hands and trying to stop the blood from my nose, which was flowing down my neck.

Anna pulled out a cigarette and started smoking standing next to me, facing the other side. Vineet was massaging his arm, and Akash's t-shirt was torn.

The seniors asked Rahul to clean my blood, while I remained silent with tears in my eyes. I was feeling sorry because of what I had done just a few minutes back, but I could not control my anger.

I continued, "You called me your friend, but you are trying to spoil my relationship. I love her a lot, more than anything in this world, and if I lose her because of you all, I will never forgive you."

Vineet then came close and hugged me. "Sorry, Bhai, we are sorry. Will you not forgive your friends?"

I tried to push him back, but he caught hold of me. A hug from a friend is one of the best things in life, and I realized it that day. I hugged him tight and said sorry too. Looking at us, Akash jumped on us and so did Anna, Rahul, and all others on that floor. I got sandwiched between the hugs, and forgot about the blood and pain.

As we stood up, Vineet teased me again saying, "Vaidehi, you attacked me hard with that plate."

This time, I smiled. I understood they couldn't stop teasing me, but at least they promised that they would never let her know that they knew about our relationship.

I stayed in the mess for some time. Rahul stayed back. We pulled one bench to the corner of the terrace and sat looking at the road.

He asked me, "Do you want to talk about Vaidehi?"

I kept looking in front and replied, "I was wrong today. I was not angry with you all. I was upset with myself. I could not keep up my promise."

Rahul listened and then replied after thinking for a while. "As far as I know Vaidehi, she is a confident and bold girl; she is not concerned about what others say about her. But yes, I feel she is egoistic."

"Egoistic? No, not at all, she is friendly," I replied. It was a new comment I had heard for her.

"See, Rohan, she is friendly with you, but for the most of us she is an egoistic girl as she has not spoken to her batch-mates even once in the last one year," Rahul explained calmly.

"I don't buy your point; she is not at all egoistic," I insisted.

Rahul was not right and I could not listen to anything against her. She was my love, and I could not let her down. It might be his prospect, but for me, she was the most loving and friendly person.

It was the day of the annual function. I took part in the dance, partnered with Chaaru while Vaidehi partnered with Akash. Mom and Papa had also come to Jabalpur for my annual function. This was the best time for me to introduce her to them.

I was backstage getting ready for the performance when the warden informed me that Papa was waiting for me in the garden area of the venue. I rushed to him and saw Mom standing with him.

I was dressed in a dhoti and a red kurta with a Punjabi turban. I touched their feet and hugged them in happiness.

"Thank you both for coming to this function," I thanked them.

"You were performing; we had to come to see," Mom replied, stroking my head.

Papa, who was still looking at me lovingly, pulled out something from the bag he was holding.

"This is for you Rohan," he said as he handed me a box wrapped in gift paper.

Surprised, I opened the gift and saw a black Kodak camera. "Wow Papa, I love you. This is what I always wanted!"

Papa smiled and patted me on my back. I could now capture every moment of my college life with Vaidehi. I thanked him again and asked for their leave as my performance was about to start. I asked them to take the front seat, so they could see me perform better.

On my way to the backstage, I entered the sitting area where the students were seated. My eyes were searching for Anurag. He was not performing, but could help me by taking pictures of my performance with my new camera.

I handed him my camera and asked him to take our pictures.

Soon our performance started, and we rocked the show. I could see Papa enjoying it a lot. There were many shows, and once we finished our performance, we changed and returned to the students' sitting area.

Vaidehi took a seat next to me, and we both enjoyed the rest of the show, shouting, laughing and hooting. Anurag had taken many pictures by then and handed over my camera to me.

I could see Papa and Mom sitting in front. I came close to Vaidehi's ears to speak as it was noisy. "Come, let me introduce you to my parents."

She looked shocked "Really? You want me to meet them?"

"Obviously, I will introduce you as a friend only. At least they would remember you when I'll tell them about our relationship after college." I explained to her, while she listened me bringing her ear close to me.

She was looking gorgeous that day. Beautiful girls with make-up on their faces look ethereal. I could not stop staring at her.

I caught her hand and asked her to get up, and we moved to the front row to meet my parents. She was looking more beautiful in fear.

"Should I touch their feet?" she asked me softly. I smiled at her. "I love you, this matters a lot for me...touching feet of my parents is your call."

"Mom, she is Vaidehi," I introduced her. Mom and Papa stood up from their seat when we approached.

Vaidehi folded her hands in a namaste and then moved down to touch their feet.

Papa stopped her by saying, "Let it be, it's not required, beta."

Mom was looking at her with happy eyes as though she would take her home that very moment. As there was nothing much to talk about, I informed Papa that I would be with my friends and would reach the hostel late. They could leave for our relative's house where they were staying. I took their leave, and Vaidehi finally relaxed. We moved back to our seats and enjoyed the show.

After a few minutes, she asked me to follow her. She stood up and went outside, avoiding the mob of students who were shouting. I stood up once she left and followed her.

As I reached outside, it was dark. It was 8:30 p.m. I looked around, but could not find her. I went towards the garden and saw her standing in the middle of the lawn, all alone.

I went up and stood behind her, "What happened love?" I asked coming closer to her.

She kept looking at the stars that filled in night sky, "This is the first time we are together at night."

I moved to her side and held her hand. She entangled her fingers in mine. Her pink suit was shining brightly in the moonlight.

"First time I saw your hair open, like the night sky, you looked so beautiful," I added.

"Look at those two stars, shining bright, like they want to tell us a story of their love," she replied, and I added, "but their voices are not reaching us."

She turned her head down and turned to me, "I wanted to spend time with you."

"I want to spend every moment with you," I confirmed.

She was looking so beautiful in the moonlight that I wanted to kiss her. It was quiet there with everyone busy watching the show, while we love birds were enjoying each other's company. The blooming flowers in the garden added to the atmosphere.

"You love me, or is it a myth?" I asked her.

"Remember one thing, whatever happens in the future, I will love you till my death," she replied looking deep into my eyes.

I held her hand and said, "Let's move inside."

She asked me, "Why? Aren't you liking it here?"

I looked deep into her eyes. "This is the most romantic and memorable moment of my life. Will remember this time till my last breath. You are one of the best gifts god has given me in my life, but if I stay with you any longer, I might kiss you. Before my heart takes its course, let's move inside." I took hold of her hand and started walking, but she kept standing and pulled my hand back.

As I turned to her, she was standing with her eyes closed. Her hair was blowing with the breeze, along with the ends of her dupatta. She didn't want to go back to the auditorium. I moved closer to her and placed my right hand on her waist, moved my left hand over her right cheeks and came close to her. She kept her eyes closed, waiting for a kiss. Her fragrance was overwhelming. I touched her glossy lips with my fingers and put my lips on hers. The peck converted to a long kiss.

I cupped her cheek that was slowly turning red. I smiled at her before slowly leaning towards her. My other hand was shaking slightly, my mind was repeating the same sentence over and over, "I love you... I love you." But the sound of my heart beating so loudly made it difficult to concentrate. Finally, my lips touched her lips again. Sparks flew in every direction, and the world was slowly disappearing around us, along with all of our worries. She made me feel like none of that mattered. I honestly never knew a kiss could be so intimate and electrifying. Her lips were moving in perfect sync as my hands felt her waist. I pulled her closer and the kiss turned more passionate. I felt her hands on the back of my neck play with the ends of my hair. A smile grew on my face as it started to tickle. Finally, we pulled apart.

She opened her eyes the next minute and spoke softly, "I love you and will always love you. You found parts of me I didn't know existed, and in you, I found love I no longer believed was real."

That was the moment I understood how much she loved me and how much I loved her.

Being loved by someone gives you strength, while loving someone gives you courage. Love is that condition in which the happiness of another person is as essential as your own.

She told me one more thing as we made our way back, "Even though I'm unsure about most things in life, I am certain I love you and will continue to love you forever."

I smiled at her words and kissed her on her forehead.

She felt confident after meeting my parents. Maybe she now believed I truly loved her. Her kiss in the open garden area was a sign that she truly and deeply was in love with me.

Sometimes I feel I didn't really understand her, but I only want to love her, without knowing why I loved her so much.

Present day, 2003

It was 11:30 p.m. when I entered Dehradun. I was so lost in the memories of Vaidehi that I didn't remember how the four hours had passed. I felt like I was back in college and she was waiting for me in Jabalpur. But reality was different. I was alone at night on an empty ISBT road in Dehradun. As we were crossing Chandrabani Chowk, I asked Rajesh to stop the car.

He nodded and lowered the speed, switched on the parking lights and stopped by the side of the road. "Is everything okay sir?" Rajesh asked, turning back to me.

"Haan, just need to buy a cigarette packet," I replied.

I stepped out and went across to the tiny paan shop at the corner of the road, which was still open. I pulled out my purse and asked him for a Gold Flake cigarette pack. Rajesh opened the car bonnet and checked the water level. I pulled out one cigarette and leaned against the back of the car. I took a puff and thought about that evening in the hostel when I had got a call from Papa.

I was having fun with friends in the hostel when someone shouted my name. There was a phone call for me.

I ran downstairs to attend the call. The STD booth owner, who hardly smiled, asked me to wait as my papa would give a call back. I wondered why Papa had called me and hoped everything was okay. He hardly called me. The phone rang, and I bent to pick it up.

"There is good news, Rohan." Papa informed me in excitement. I could hear Mom murmuring; she was excited to talk to me.

"What happened Papa?" I asked him with a smile on my face, hearing his excitement.

"Surbhi' s marriage date is finalized. It's ten days from today."

That was great news. I was happy for my sister; she would start a new life now.

"Wow! That's great. Where is she?" I asked. Papa informed me she was out shopping with her close friends and would be late. I asked him to congratulate her on my behalf and that I'd call her again tomorrow.

"Lot of work needs to be done; you try to come home at least a week before," Mom said, snatching the phone from Papa.

"Ya sure Mom, I will."

She continued expressing her excitement. "I will courier some invitation cards which you can distribute to your friends in college and ask all your friends to come."

Hearing this, I got an idea. I asked her to give the receiver to Papa.

"Papa, can you book the Sangam Hotel in Civil Lines for some of my friends," I requested him.

"Why not? Let me know how many rooms and I'll book," he replied.

I was planning to invite some of my close friends to Surbhi Di's wedding, including Vaidehi. The idea was to introduce her to my entire family. She would also have time to meet my family and understand them. Hope this would break the ice and she'd accept our relationship openly. I understand it was not important that we behave like a couple in front of others, but at least that fear of getting noticed should be absent.

But I was not sure if she would come to the wedding or not. Her attitude was tough to understand.

I knew if I would ask her to come for the wedding, she might say no, in concern of getting noticed. So, I devised a plan to get her to agree. As I received the invitation cards, I invited some of her close friends, ignoring her. My aim was to get Chaaru to agree to visit Sagar for my sister's wedding. I knew, if I had to make her jealous, I needed to flirt with Chaaru. Since the annual function performance, she had been feeling insecure, as I had partnered with Chaaru. I was hoping my plan would work.

On that day when I reached college, Chaaru and Reena were sitting outside with Vaidehi. Reena was also our batch-mate, a studious and silent girl. Chaaru and Reena were discussing something about studies while Vaidehi was busy reading my poems in my old silver diary. She had taken the diary during our annual function day when I had brought it to recite some lines during the show. She was not aware that I had reached her and was standing next to her.

I was all set to start my plan to make her jealous. "Hi Chaaru and Reena," I greeted them pulling out invitation cards from my bag. They replied with a smile. Vaidehi looked towards me, with a smile. I smiled at her and then showed my beatific face to Chaaru, "This is for you," I passed an invitation card to her and one to Reena.

"What is this? Who is getting married?" Reena asked me opening the card. I could see the anxious look on Vaidehi's face. I was smiling inside.

"My sister Surbhi is getting married next week. You all must come. Sagar is just a five-hour drive from Jabalpur," I coaxed them.

Vaidehi closed the diary with a thud, stood up, pulled her bag on her shoulder and started walking away, showing no interest in my conversation with Chaaru and Reena, giving me a wolfish look. I noticed her movement and followed her. After a few long steps, I was on her side. "Will you be coming to Sagar for Surbhi Di's wedding?"

She stopped and gave a Mona Lisa smile. I loved that smile. "You miss Navya a lot?" she asked me with a cruel smile.

"I only love you," I replied with a quizzical look.

"She is all over in the three hundred and twenty-six poems you have written," she confirmed with exact figures, which even I had not noticed.

"You read all of them?" I replied with an astonished face.

"Hardly matters," she said and began walking again, while I followed her. Why are girls so complicated? She knew I had liked Navya before I met her, so I would have written those poems for her. Now, I love her and would write more poems for her.

"So are you coming to the wedding?" I suddenly asked. She thought for a while and then replied looking into my eyes, "On two conditions: one, if the others are going; and second, if you take me to places where you spent time with Navya."

The first condition I could understand, as she would require convincing her family, but the second one was weird. What would she do visiting those places where I used to meet Navya and that is obviously, my school. But when she looked into my eyes, I could only say what she wanted me to say, and I replied "Okay done. Vineet is planning to book a bus for all classmates who would like to join. They'd reach Sagar by the afternoon and next morning would return to Jabalpur. I've got rooms booked in the hotel."

"And what about the second and more essential condition?" she insisted.

"Although I am not interested in visiting my school, I'll take you there as you are insisting," I said. She gave a mischievous smile and left.

Soon, I distributed the invitation cards to almost all my friends, and most of them confirmed that they would come. I would be leaving almost a week early, and so Vineet and Thakur took the responsibility to arrange the bus and ensure to bring everyone.

I was really excited to have Vaidehi come to my hometown. I wanted her to meet Surbhi Di as she had not met her earlier. Also, it was such an amazing feeling to have a complete family together, yes Vaidehi was family by then.

On the day of Surbhi Di' s wedding, I was leaving for Sindhi Market in Sagar to collect Didi's lehenga, when Papa informed me that there was a call from Sangam Hotel that my guests had arrived. I dropped in at the hotel to check if all the arrangements were in order and my friends were comfortable there. I rode my scooty to the hotel. I saw Vineet, Anna and Thakur standing in the corner, smoking. I went up to them with a smile. We hugged, and I thanked them for coming.

"Let us know if you need any help; we will get it done," Thakur said. I thanked them, asked them to rest for some time and then get ready by six as the baraat would arrive early.

While they were still smoking, I asked them to excuse me as I wanted to meet Vaidehi. It had been five days since I had seen her. I took the stairs to the first floor. I entered the reception and had a word with the manager to check whether all the arrangements had been made. I proceeded to welcome all my friends from Jabalpur.

I entered room number 107; I knocked the door which was already open and saw my love standing along with Chaaru and

Reena, busy discussing the jewelry which they were planning to wear to the function.

"Hi Rohan, I was expecting you with a welcome card at the hotel gate when I arrived," Vaidehi said as soon as she saw me. I smiled at her,

"Oh! I am sorry, I should have done that, but it's never too late," I replied and picked up a powder bottle, dusted some powder on my hand and put a tilak of powder on her forehead. We all laughed loudly while she slapped me on my shoulder. "Hope your journey was comfortable," I asked them.

Chaaru confirmed that the journey was great and the hotel was fabulous. I asked them to have lunch which was arranged in the common area and requested they excuse Vaidehi for some time. "Where are you pulling me, Rohan?" she asked me while coming out of the room.

I took her out and looked at her eyes, "Let me have a look, it's been five days since I have seen you." She smiled and gave me a radiant look.

"Expect nothing more than this," she warned with a smile.

I smiled and turned off my roguish look. "Will you join me shopping?" I asked her.

"Where?"

"I am going to collect the lehenga for my sister, why don't you join me?" I said. With a beatific expression, she started walking along with me. We reached the parking area. "Oh, a scooty!"

"Would you like to drive?" I asked her, handing over the keys to her.

She took the keys from my hand with a naughty smile and replied, "Today, Mr Rohan, you will be famous in your city, riding behind the most beautiful girl in town."

I gave a shy look and sat behind her. She was excited to drive on the new roads. She kept on asking me the directions while my eyes were on people whom I knew, who were looking at me with curiosity. After crossing heavy traffic of the Sagar primary market, we reached Sindhi Market.

Sindhi Market was famous for girl's clothes and accessories, and she was looking around bug-eyed. We took the narrow roads with girls' suits and saris on both sides. We reached the shop, from which I needed to pick up the lehenga. "Is it ready, bhaiya?" I asked store owner. He nodded while looking at her and packed the lehenga.

"Wait, let me check it first," she interrupted the man who was packing it and looked at it.

"It's wonderful, your sister would look beautiful in red colour," she replied, placing it on her body. I looked at her and hoped that the day comes soon when she would wear such a lehenga for me. As Papa had already paid for it, I took it, and we rode back to the hotel. As we reached Civil Lines, where the hotel was, I asked her, "Would like to have the famous gol gappas of Sagar?"

She was excited and agreed. She sat behind me and kept her hand on my shoulder. I looked at her sideways and smiled. We reached Bharat Chat Centre, one of the famous chat corners in Sagar.

We took our plates, and she opened her mouth wide, to put a gol gappa in, in one shot. Her eyes widened and the tears reflected the spicy taste. After one, I stopped and asked him to keep serving her. I just wanted to watch her. How could someone be so beautiful? Her every move was mesmerizing me. I got lost in her; she touched me with her elbow to ask where I was lost. I nodded softly, smiling. She was smiling and gestured to me that she loved the taste. For a moment, I felt it was a scene from the movie, and everything was happening in slow motion.

We returned to the hotel. Vineet and Thakur were still downstairs. Vaidehi ran upstairs, and I told Vineet to reach the venue by six. I said that I would be busy and may not attend to them, but they must feel comfortable. I handed over the address to them on a slip of paper and returned home.

I went straight to Surbhi Di, she was busy getting the mehndi done on her hands. My sister was looking perfect that day. I looked at her and remembered how we used to fight to get the gold medal. From today onwards, a new relationship would start, which would be more mature. We'd understand each other's feelings much better. I pulled out her lehenga from the plastic bag and kept in front of her. "Your Lehenga! Check if it's okay or needs alteration." She looked happy.

"Wow, it's looking perfect, brother. Thanks." As I got up to tackle other tasks, she asked, "Where is Vaidehi?"

I stopped, turned and replied, "She is in the hotel and will come in the evening."

"Oh! You should have brought her. I would have loved to meet her. I wanted to see what a nymph she is."

I smiled. "Don't worry, she will meet you for sure. You think about Anuj."

I felt emotional and hugged her. "Don't do this, Rohan. If I cry, my make-up will get spoiled."

I left, with tears in my eyes.

It was evening time and and the guests had already turned up at the venue. Papa and Mummy were dressed up and were at the venue to welcome the guests, along with a few of my relatives. Everything was ready for the big fat wedding to start. I dressed up in my navy blue solid single breasted formal suit, with a blue printed tie. As I entered the venue to check the arrangements,

Papa smiled at me and hugged me. "My son has grown up to a handsome man now," he said proudly.

I smiled at him and hugged him, "Thanks Papa."

In front was the stage decorated with beautiful white and red flowers, with a big red sofa in between, on which the bride and groom would be seated. By then, guests had already come and were sitting in the front row. The music from the shehnai filled the evening.

As predicted by Vaidehi, Surbhi Di was glowing in the red lehenga. She was looking like the perfect bride, with jewellery and make-up. By that time, many guests had already arrived, but my eyes were searching for the most beautiful girl in this world – Vaidehi.

I was busy getting the garland arranged for the groom, who would reach the venue any moment when I saw Vaidehi entering from the main entrance. She looked radiant in a purple and pink lehenga. I could not blink my eyes looking at her. I was staring at her when she smiled at me. She was looking out of this world.

She waved her hand at me with a big smile and then gestured showing okay with her fingers when suddenly I saw Navya entering behind her. My smile faded.

Navya was a cousin of Surbhi Di's friend, and she had accompanied her. My eyes went to her while I was waving at Vaidehi. Navya was looking beautiful, wearing a yellow and black suit. Vaidehi noticed my eyes and smile, and turned back to check whom I was looking at. My eyes were back on Vaidehi, ignoring Navya. I pretended I had not seen Navya, whereas Navya had seen me and gave a tiny smile. Vaidehi had never seen Navya, not even her picture. She didn't know who I was looking at. I was in a dilemma as I was facing the one whom I love the most and the one whom I had loved the most.

Vaidehi smiled coming closer to me and spoke in my ears, "Mr Rohan, I never knew you could be so handsome."

I held her hand and replied, "And I was not aware that I had the most beautiful girl of the universe as my girlfriend." She gave me a radiant look.

I saw Navya moving to another side with her cousin and take a seat next to the stage. I wondered if I should go to Navya and have a word with her. I was never sure if Navya ever knew about my feelings for her.

I asked Vaidehi and my other friends to take a seat while I moved to the main entrance as the baraat had arrived. I ran and stood beside my parents. Anuj looked handsome in a sherwani. He smiled at me. Anuj' s friends and relatives were still dancing. We offered garlands to welcome them and asked them to sit.

In some time, the rituals started. Anuj sat on the sofa on the stage. Now it was time for Surbhi Di to come to the stage. I rushed to her at the entrance and took hold of the long *chunari* which was supposed to be held at each corner by four people. The bride would have to walk under it.

I was holding the corner on the left to Surbhi Di in front of her. She started walking a few steps and then stopped. She brought her face near my ears and asked me to call Vaidehi to hold the other corner. I smiled at her concern and went to Vaidehi, making my cousin hold my end. I ran towards her and spoke in her ears about what Surbhi Di had requested. She smiled and started walking along with me. As we reached her, Vaidehi smiled and spoke bringing her face near Di's, "Didi, you are looking gorgeous." I was happy to see her communicating with my sister. I took the end I had been holding, and Vaidehi took hold of the end next to me. We started walking along, with the same speed and steps. I turned right to look at her, she smiled at me and looked into my eyes. I smiled back. As we reached the stage, I could see Navya standing with her cousin and clapping at the entry of the bride.

Navya looked into my eyes and smiled. I smiled back and moved ahead. We took Surbhi Di on stage for the *varmala*. I stood next to Vaidehi when the ritual started. Everyone was cheering and clapping, when Vaidehi slightly pinched my hand. I looked at her and smiled. She gestured to me to see and learn the rituals. I slightly pushed her with my shoulder to the side and she pushed me back.

While we were enjoying the ritual, my eyes fell on Navya, who was observing me, pained. I stopped smiling and tried to ignore her.

After the rituals were over, I asked all my friends to proceed towards the dining area and requested Vaidehi to excuse me as I had to attend to a few guests. I walked straight to Navya as she was standing at the corner, waiting for coffee. "Hello Navya, how are you?" I asked her. She turned to me and smiled with a grave expression "I am good, how are you?"

"I am fine too."

And then there was a pause for one minute between both us and then she spoke. "I was expecting you would talk to me about something."

I was expressionless and wanted to tell her that things had changed, but I didn't want to hurt her. But why I was worried? I did not know whether she liked me or not.

I thought it was better not to show that I was ever attracted to her and changed the topic. "So, how are your Pharma classes going?"

"Okay, good I'll say," she replied and then again there was this awkward silence, which then she broke. "Who is that girl with you?"

I looked grave and didn't know what to say. If I said she was just my friend, it would be a lie, and Navya may have hope; and if I told her she was my girlfriend, she might lash out. After thinking for a while, I thought it was better to be straightforward.

"She is my girlfriend Vaidehi," I said confidently. She heard it and gave a sardonic smile.

"I should go; my cousin is waiting for me," she replied with a sullen face.

I smiled and gave way. She walked without looking into my eyes and then stopped, turned and replied, "Rohan, you know a heart has many feelings which are kept buried in the depth of it, and it's someone among many, who brings them out. Hope you can be truthful with her because when feelings get hurt, your life gets affected."

I kept looking at her, and she kept looking into my eyes for a few seconds. Then she left without turning back.

Each person has his or her destiny written in heaven. I had heard this, but felt it for the first time in my life. Navya loved me, and if I had proposed to her in school, she would have accepted it, and maybe I would have never met Vaidehi then. Destiny wanted Vaidehi and me to be together, and so all this happened. I was much relaxed.

The girl whom I had loved like crazy for years was leaving in front of my eyes, but there was no regret.

Navya

Hi, I am Navya. I guess I must not have been part of Rohan's memories. I want to write bad things about him, but I still love him. Maybe till the end of my life, I will love him for his innocence.

When I first met him in school, I never knew I would fall in love with him. But the way he interacted with me and respected every girl in school, I fell in love with him. I have always seen love in his eyes. He used to come to school daily, even when his batch-mates had stopped, just to meet me, but I think he never noticed that I too came just to meet him.

I always knew he called me to listen to my voice and then disconnected the line, but he never knew I had a caller Id installed and whenever he called, why it was only me who picked up his call. The last time I saw him before he left for Jabalpur, outside the school with Vikram, I wanted him to come and propose to me, but he never did.

When he called me from his hostel, I was expecting he would propose, but he stopped again that day. Maybe it was destiny which stopped me from proposing to him and destiny stopped him from proposing to me.

Relations get set in heaven, and this was proved. I loved him, and he loved me, but still, we can never be together in life.

I remember once he gave me his physics book in school to study, in which he had kept a poem he had written. He told me the next day that it was by mistake that he had left it in the book but he never noticed how much I had liked it.

He only saw what he wanted to see; he only made rules for himself. He wrote his own story without realizing I was also a part of it.

I will not be part of his life anymore, but he can never erase the time and memories which he has spent with me. I wish that he and Vaidehi stay blessed forever.

One day, if we meet again, I hope to see both of them smiling as I saw them today. I looked at them with sad eyes, but deep in my heart, I was thrilled for my friend Rohan. He had found someone wonderful for himself. May god help me to find someone wonderful too.

Time is too slow for those who wait,
Too swift for those who fear,
Too long for those who grieve,
Too short for those who rejoice,
But for those who love,
Time is an eternity.
Will love you forever Rohan.

Your incomplete girlfriend,
Navya

It was midnight and the ceremonies were going on. I was sitting with my friends from college, including Vaidehi. Papa and Mom were sitting beside Surbhi Di, who was performing rituals in front of the sacred fire along with Anuj.

We were chatting and laughing loudly. I was thankful to them for coming. Anurag was telling us stories of his uncles and making us laugh a lot.

Vaidehi stood up from the chair she was sitting on and walked towards a quiet area and gestured to me to join her. I asked my friends to excuse me. I stood up, holding my blazer on my shoulder and went to her. She kept walking outside the main entrance, and I followed her. It was silent outside. I reached her and walked beside her.

"You promised me something, Rohan," she spoke, looking at me.

"Did I forget something?" I asked her puzzled.

"You said you would show me places where you met Navya," she replied.

"Ah! I remember," I responded with a sigh. I looked at the venue, wondering if I could bunk the rituals. "Okay, come let's go," I replied taking out the keys of my scooty.

"Are you sure?" she asked. By that time, I had pulled out my scooty.

"C'mon Miss Sharma, your driver is waiting."

She smiled and jumped to the back seat of the scooty. I smiled and said naughtily, "I am a persistent brake user." She slapped me on my head.

"Driver, look in front and drive," she ordered with a mischievous smile on her face.

It was a most memorable drive with empty roads, pleasant weather, the silence of love, and twinkling stars above. I checked her in the mirror of the scooty as she held my shoulders from behind. She was looking beautiful. As we were moving towards my school, I leaned back and spoke, "I love you." She smiled shyly. She hugged me this time and kept her left cheek on my shoulder.

In the next fifteen minutes, we were at the main gate of our school. It was a fifty-meter lane from the main entrance to the main building of the school. We entered through a small passage in the gate and walked on the lane which was lined with trees on both sides. This was one of the most memorable places in my school, from where we entered the institution every day.

"This is the lane where I used to follow Navya every day when school ended while walking to our buses," I told her about the first place, which was memorable. She looked at me with a thoughtful expression. We walked further, but soon she took long steps to move ahead of me and replied without looking at me, "Along this lane you followed Navya, now follow me. " And she walked faster with a mischievous smile. I followed her.

After crossing the lane, we reached the main administration building. There was a huge statue of Jesus Christ with his arms spread to hug his followers. She stood in front of it and prayed with closed eyes.

"Along with admin building, is the hostel for sisters and nuns, who stay here only, so let's move from here. We will be kicked out if someone comes to know we have entered school at night," I said. The school was looking different in the night; it was really quiet. We reached the assembly area. I walked towards the stage in the corner, holding her hand. "This is the stage, where every morning, we used to have our prayers, and this is the place, where I saw Navya for the first time. I was standing on stage, and she walked from that side." I turned to show her from where she had walked, pointing my finger. She kept listening with a thoughtful look and then replied, "Rohan, can you please stand in the same place where you stood that day."

With a quizzical look on my face, I listened to her and climbed on the stage, while she kept observing me. "This was the place I stood that day," I confirmed. With a set smile, she moved to the position from where Navya had come out. She reached that point and then sighed, turned and walked taking the same path Navya had taken years back. She walked towards me, while my eyes were on her moves. She walked boldly, looking gorgeous and came near. "Is this how she came?" she questioned.

I was lost in her eyes and didn't reply. She asked again, "Is this how she came on stage?"

"Maybe," I replied murmuring.

She smiled. "Now show me the other places also."

I did not understand what she was up to, but I was enjoying those moments with her.

"Yes, let's move to the other side." I took her to the next side of the building, where we had a big auditorium. We walked along the long corridor and reached the auditorium. "Vaidehi, come from here, this door seems to be open."

The auditorium was huge, with almost a two thousand seating capacity. I switched on the lights. She took a complete circle to admire its beauty. In front of the auditorium was a big stage. I stood in front of it and told her, "This is the stage on which I performed with Navya."

She took a few steps and came near hands folded, a soft smile on her face and looked at the stage. Her eyes showed she was in deep thoughts. She went to the centre of the stage. She opened her bag which she was carrying on her shoulder and pulled out a Walkman. She placed her bag on the side of the auditorium and asked me to come over. I did, while she inserted a cassette in the Walkman and put on her earphones. As I reached to her, she gave a sly smile and placed one ear plug into my left ear and another ear plug into her right ear. As the earphone cord was not too long, we stayed close to each other; I could feel her breath. I was quizzical and looked into her eyes. She then switched on the Walkman. After a few seconds, the song from the movie *Khamoshi* played, '*Bahon ke dermiyaan, do pyaar mil rahe hain.*' As it started, I gestured to her with my eyes, "Now what?"

She took my right hand and placed it on her waist while holding my left hand. She moved her legs slowly. She was trying to dance slowly with me. There was silence all around, but the most romantic song was playing in our ears. We danced to the rhythm, feeling each other. She looked confident and shy while I was nervous. As she turned, her silky hair touched my face. Our hands moved and legs danced.

It was the most mesmerizing moment for me. I was in the best part of life.

She pulled her head up again and looked at me, switching off the song, still holding my hands. "What memories you will carry of your school in future, Rohan?" she asked me with a grave look.

I looked into her eyes and replied, with a pause, "I will remember this night till my death."

She smiled and looked relaxed. I looked at her and asked kissing her palm, "What were you trying to do?"

Her face was glowing, she smiled and picked up her bag, "From today onwards, whenever you will recall your school, you will only remember me."

I kept listening to her. "I cannot share your memories with Navya," she added.

I kept looking at her in surprise and went to hug her when someone opened the door of the auditorium. "Who's there?" I turned to check and saw one of the sisters from the school administration with a torch in her hand.

"Oh shit! We need to run Vaidehi," I said and caught hold of her hand and pulled her to run on another side of the auditorium. We started running with the beam of the torchlight following us. We ran to the door on the other side of the stage, and luckily found it open. We yelled, laughed and ran, while sister was shouting at us to stop. "Run Vaidehi, we cannot stop!"

We ran through the corridor and our footsteps echoed in the silent school premises.

"Guard, guard, where are you? Catch these intruders!" Sister shouted from behind. But we had reached the lane to the main gate while running hand in hand. I turned and saw the guards coming running behind us. We moved faster. Vaidehi was still laughing loudly; she was enjoying the chase. We went out of the gate and rushed to our scooty. Guards almost reached us while I was trying to plug in the keys.

"Rohan, start fast, they are coming!" Vaidehi cried, pressing my shoulders. The guards reached the gate when our scooty finally started and we made our escape.

We were laughing at the craziest thing we had done that night. "Oh my god, that was crazy!" she said from behind, still laughing. After a while, I turned to check if someone was following us. I stopped the scooty when I was sure no one was. She stood on the side and we both laughed loudly, holding our stomachs. We both tried to stop laughing, but burst into giggles looking at each other's faces.

Suddenly, I stopped laughing, came close to her and held her hand. I looked into her eyes, while she was still smiling. In the silence of the city, I spoke, "Each of us has a spark of life inside us, and our highest endeavour is to set off that spark in one another. You are my spark Vaidehi, never let my spark go dull."

She stopped laughing and replied. "Love is another name for faith and laughter is the beginning of prayer. You will be in every prayer I'll say."

We both kept looking at each other's eyes as the moonlit clouds drifted across the dark sky. The sky above was full of tumultuous dark and ragged clouds. It was a night with a dull sky threatening rain. A cloud, ominous and black, drifted over the sky and released a sudden shower.

Vaidehi moved her head closer. I stood frozen, from both fear and excitement. She leaned in, so her forehead rested against mine. We closed our eyes. Water droplets ran down my eyelids. "Thank you," she said in a whisper.

"For what?" I replied, my voice low and husky.

"For being you." Her voice shook exhilarated from the love and affection between us.

She gently leaned in and kissed my warms lips. We pulled apart and took shaky, shallow breaths. Unable to contain ourselves anymore, I held her head in my hands and pulled her into a fiery and passionate kiss. Her hands worked their way around my body, feeling each line along my physique.

My hands venture over her curved body, exploring. We pulled apart and opened our eyes. We stared at each other, deep into each other's eyes. I was full of wonder and love while she was full of curiosity and passion. No words were spoken, but a story worthy of us communicated.

I leaned in and softly kissed up her neck. She let out little whimpers of anticipation. I worked my way back to her tender, smooth lips.

"Rohan," she whispered softly, prolonging each letter as if to savour them. I smiled, my heart fluttering at her voice as I clasped my hands on either side of her face. Never had my name ever sounded so beautiful. I leaned in for another kiss.

We pulled apart and opened our eyes. We stared at each other, hesitating and shy. "I think we are getting late and we are drenched."

She nodded with a radiant smile.

We started our scooty and drove back to the venue where the rituals were almost over and it was time to say adieu to my sister.

I heard my mom weeping and telling Surbhi Di, "Marriage isn't a ritual in front of god, or a paper signed. It is the union of two hearts beating as one, each that would sacrifice for the other's happiness and well-being. Marriage is the blessing we give to one another, an eternal bond of soul-mates."

My eyes filled up.

Anurag Thakur

What can be more amazing for two souls in love than an assurance that they are there for each other in pain. Rohan was my best friend or you can say he was my second family, my brother. We met for the first time in college, and we became friends instantly. Friends without benefits and expectations. Rohan was a guy whom I will define as sincere, calm and sorted. He always tried to understand his friends before giving his opinion, and that was what was best about him.

He was a jerk though, and I feel every boy is a jerk, but he was sincere in his love. He told me once he loved the girl in his school Navya, but when he fell in love with Vaidehi and understood that his feelings for Navya were not love but infatuation, he never cheated on Vaidehi.

I still remember, once when we were having tea at the corner shop in Gorakhpur, he showed concern about his hostel friends, who made fun of his relation with Vaidehi. Although he knew Vaidehi was a sensible girl and she understood the teasing nature of friends, he was more concerned for slander.

He was an energetic boy and loved his parents a lot. He'd never go against them, but it was sure that his parents would never create a situation for him to go against them.

I was shocked when I went to Sagar along with him and saw how open his parents were. They never objected to discussing girls. Even after so much freedom, he was a one-girl man.

Coming back to Vaidehi... I had known her since the last four years. She was the most beautiful girl in Jabalpur. Bold, talented, upfront and damn beautiful. Christ Church Girls School is one of the most famous schools in Jabalpur and produces some of the best, good looking and talented girls. And who can hide a girl like Vaidehi? She was the dream girl for every other boy from most of the schools in Jabalpur.

But apart from this, she was famous for her attitude and arrogant nature. But I didn't agree. If a girl is not entertaining your request, it doesn't mean she's arrogant.

Rohan and Vaidehi were two different people, but someone has proved in the past that negative and positive attract. So, they were together. I was always worried for Rohan because if she dumped him, he would be broken.

I considered myself as Rohan's best friend, but the truth is that I could never be with him during college hours. Vaidehi was too possessive about him. During college, Rohan sat next to her, he ate his tiffin with her, he attended practical classes with her, and he only chatted with her in his free time, and finally, he dropped her home. Rohan did not realize it, but he was losing friends, or you may say, he was not making any friends.

I felt that I mustn't be his friend as he didn't need one. Vaidehi and Rohan were made for each other, and there was no space between them. Rohan was losing his hostel mates as well.

I don't know if he was correct, or whether Vaidehi was perfect, but I felt I was losing a wonderful friend while he was blooming in a garden called love. For me, he was always my best friend, and for him, I will always be there.

I was in Sagar during the holidays, after my second semester. The next day, I would be returning to Jabalpur as my third semester was about to start.

We had been invited by Surbhi Di for dinner that day. As she also lived in Sagar, I'd often visit her during the holidays. That day Anuj Jiju invited me for dinner as he had made mutton for me. I heard he cooked delicious food but hadn't got a chance to taste any yet. I was excited about the dinner.

By seven in the evening, we reached her house. Papa and Mom took their scooter while I followed them on my scooty. I hated to ride that pink scooty that had belonged to Surbhi Di before her marriage, but Papa was not ready to buy me a bike.

"Welcome hero, on your pink scooty," Anuj opened the door and welcomed us.

"One day, I'll paint it at night," I retorted with a deadpan expression and entered his sweet home. Surbhi Di came out running and hugged me.

"Are you still cooking? Need help?" Mom asked my sister.

"No, everything is ready Mom. It's Anuj who is still cooking. I was just helping him."

The house was filled with the aroma of mutton. We made ourselves comfortable. I could not resist entering the kitchen to take a peek at the mutton.

"Haan! It looks mind blowing. I am so hungry," I said.

"Give me a few more minutes; it will be ready soon," Anuj replied while stirring the mutton and continued in a mischievous tone. "Have your fill, as I don't think in a few years' time you will be able to have non-veg food."

I gave a confused look. "Why?"

"Vaidehi is Brahmin, I suppose," he replied teasing.

I smiled and replied, "You are Brahmin too, Jiju, and you're making mutton."

We laughed, and I returned to the drawing room and sat next to my sister.

"Which semester will you start now?" Surbhi Di asked me.

"Third," I replied, lost in my thoughts as I thought about the journey the next day. I had observed a change in my thoughts since I had met Vaidehi.

I was at a dinner at my sister's home, but my mind and heart were with Vaidehi.

Anuj came and sat next to Papa and discussed politics while Mom helped Surbhi Di and went to the kitchen along with her.

I was planning my next day in college. I had bought new t-shirts and jeans, as now we didn't have to adhere to the dress code of the first year. I got a new hairstyle and had got new Woodland shoes. I did not want to miss a single chance to impress her. I knew she loved me and it was important that I didn't let her down. We made a perfect pair – I was 5 feet 10 inches tall, and she was five feet six inches tall with a perfect figure.

I was missing her a lot, especially seeing my sister and Anuj happily married. "Papa, I'll be right back," I stood up and informed my father.

He looked at me, putting the newspaper down, and asked. "Where are you going?"

"Nothing, just getting bored so going for a walk."

"Okay, but come fast," he told me and I left. I wanted to call Vaidehi as I was missing her a lot, but making a call from Surbhi Di' s house would not be a good idea. I went to the STD booth, which was at the corner of the road.

"Is the phone free, need to call a number in Jabalpur?" I asked the STD booth owner, who was watching television. Without speaking, he pointed to the phone inside the cabin. It would be easy for me to talk to her or kiss her on the phone. I picked up the receiver to dial her number. Unlike Navya, I did not hesitate to call Vaidehi and ask for her even if someone else picked up the call.

I dialled her number. I waited, and after three rings, someone picked up. "Hello."

A female voice answered the call.

"Hello, may I talk to Vaidehi?"

She asked, "May I know who is speaking?"

"I am, Rohan, her classmate," I replied confidently, with a sly smile on my face.

Then something happened, which I had not expected.

"Rohan, let me make it clear. Vaidehi is not at all interested in talking to you. You must neither call her nor try to talk to her. Hope it's loud and clear," the voice said in anger.

I was shocked, and my breath stopped. My throat went dry, and a sudden pain shot up my head. I was not expecting what I heard; my voice choked. Sweat flowed from my forehead and I felt like there was no energy in my hands to hold the receiver.

She banged the phone down. Confused, I wondered who the person on the phone was. Was Vaidehi fine or was she in trouble? My mind stopped working. I kept sitting there for a few more minutes, wondering if I should call back again. But I decided not to. The woman sounded really angry. I stood up, opened the cabin and came out. I was so worried that I left without paying the booth vendor. He called me from behind, asking for his ten rupees. I became depressed and could hear the sound of my heart beating. I was not sure what to do, but I understood that I must not go to Surbhi Di's house in such a condition. I calmed down and went to a small park nearby and sat there on a bench.

What could have happened? Who was the person who had scolded me? Maybe she informed her father about us and he had forced her to stop talking. But if her father was having a problem, he would have taken me to the principal as he knew people in the management. Was Vaidehi bored with me and this she thought was the best way to get rid of me?

There were so many questions jumping in my mind, but I had no answers to them. A few days back, she had been in my arms, kissing me. What had happened in the last few days? I looked at the sky and recalled the last day of my second semester. We had all gone to watch *Dulhan Hum Le Jayenge*, starring Salman Khan and Karishma Kapoor, in Jyoti Talkies.

I still remember, she sat next to me in the theater, and we both watched the movie, holding hands. She felt depressed as I was leaving for home for a month. She told me she would miss me a lot.

"It's tough to stay without you," she interrupted in the middle of the movie murmuring in my ears. I pressed her palm with my hands, looked into her eyes and replied, "I will miss you a lot too."

"When you realize you want to spend the rest of your life with somebody, you want the rest of your life to start as soon as possible. And you are leaving me for a month, stupid," she said to me with her Mona Lisa smile.

I smiled at the memory but suddenly realized my body was hot. Had I got a fever? I stood up and walked back to Surbhi Di's house.

"Dinner is ready Rohan, where were you?" Anuj asked me as soon as I entered the house.

"Everyone please come to the dining table," Surbhi Di said.

I looked grave and my eyes were red. "What happened Rohan? Is all well," Papa asked me looking at my face.

"Ya Papa, everything is fine."

"No, your eyes are red and your face is pale," he again reiterated.

"I am feeling feverish," I replied. Mom immediately came forward and touched my forehead to check if it was hot. She confirmed I was having a fever. The phone call had had such an impact on me. It had struck deep into my heart and soul.

"Finish your dinner soon and rest. You have to travel tomorrow morning," Papa said frowning. "And if the fever persists, postpone your journey." I nodded, without speaking. My head was aching in tension. My mind was searching for questions and heart was trying to find answers. I wanted to cry loudly. But somewhere in my heart, I knew Vaidehi loved me a lot and this may be a prank. In my heart, I was sure she would come smiling when I would reach college the next day. There was no reason for her to stop talking. But I did not know I had entered the second half of my movie, which was going to be silent from now onwards.

It was the first day of my third semester.

I was wearing my blue jeans and white t-shirt, on which was printed a laughing smiley. But I was afraid and dull inside; I was crying in my heart, and I needed answers to my questions.

I walked inside the campus along with Vineet and Anurag. They too were looking different in jeans and t-shirts. As we walked in, my eyes searched for my love. I could not find her. Most of my classmates were standing in a group outside one of the classrooms.

"Why are we all standing here?" I asked one of my batch-mates.

"Third semester class will take place here," he replied.

I smiled at him and looked around for her. Finally I saw Vaidehi, wearing a blue suit sitting with Chaaru and Reena. *Thank god I found her.*

I rushed to her smiling, thinking she would give me a hug and welcome me back. But somehow my feet stopped short of her. I could see her sitting, and I was standing just a few steps behind her. My smile vanished, heartbeat quickened, I gasped and turned back. Something stopped me from reaching her and asking her what had happened.

When I proposed to her and was avoiding her, she had followed me and made me comfortable. I was sure, if everything was perfect and nothing had changed between us, she would come and talk. She could not stop talking suddenly. In my heart, I was a hundred percent sure that she would come to me smiling in some time. She cannot be without me, as I am incomplete without her.

I took my steps back and went to the side and sat on the bench there. I was sitting all alone, with my eyes on her. She was sitting at some distance but in a straight line from me. I pulled my bag from my shoulder and kept it aside, brooding. I was looking at her unblinking. I know she had noticed that I was sitting in front of her and was observing her unblinking.

She was in conversation with Chaaru, looking grave. It was visible from her eyes that she was getting annoyed because of me. But I kept watching her. Her face looked tense, with no smile and then our eyes met. I did not want to miss a chance and smiled. But she looked at me, glazed. There was no hint of a smile on her face. I blinked, and my smile faded, replaced by a pained expression. She stood up, picking up her books and moved to another side, with her back to me.

What had happened? I could not understand it at all. I was at home for the last one month. What mistake had I committed? Something must have happened, which I could not understand or recall.

I decided to talk to her and followed her but stopped as our Electronics ma'am had arrived and she asked everyone to come inside the class. I moved in and saw the seat next to her empty. Everyone in class knew I sat with her and so no one ever took it. I looked at her, standing at the main door. I was confused whether I should sit next to her or not. After thinking for few seconds, I decided to go ahead. She loved me, and I had no doubt about it.

She was avoiding me and seemed to be engrossed in the lesson. But I needed answers. I stood beside her, looking at her and pulled my bag from my back to sit next to her, when she suddenly, picked up all her books, which she was carrying and placed them on the seat without looking at me. But why? Why was she doing so? I was missing her love. I was missing her voice.

Insulted, I pulled my bag back on my shoulder and moved to the back seat. Everyone was sitting in pairs or with their friends, I looked around and found one empty seat. I took the stairs and reached the last seat and sat all alone.

Most of our classmates observed this change and understood that something had happened between Vaidehi and me. My eyes were on her, unblinking. I kept on writing her name in my notebook, again and again, without concentrating on what was happening in class.

After forty-five minutes, the lecture was over, and everyone stood up from their seats, chatting, laughing and talking with each other. While I kept sitting in my chair, looking at her unblinking, tense with red eyes. No one came or talked to me and I kept sitting alone, waiting.

In the past year, I was so smitten with Vaidehi and her love that I had ignored many friends. They had moved on, leaving me behind with her.

I stood from my seat and went to her, while she was packing her bag, with an annoyed face. "How are you?" I asked her with a pained look.

She did not bother to reply, but I could see how uncomfortable she was. I questioned her again, but she avoided me and responded to Chaaru, who was looking at me from behind her specs, "Chaaru, let's go to the library."

She stood up and moved when I caught hold of her hand. "I need an answer," I said in a loud voice. She twisted her hand and without looking at me, picked up her bag, books and left.

Chaaru followed her. I tried to stop her, but she kept moving, I followed and stopped at the classroom door, observing her leaving me. I could feel tears making my eyes wet. *Rohan, you can't let her go when you don't even know what your fault is.*

But I knew one thing, 'There is no remedy for love but to love more' and I would not stop loving her. I wiped my tears with my left hand and pulled my bag onto my shoulders and left the class. I was feeling lonely. Anurag and Vineet had gone to Saddar Bazar to have ice cream. I went outside the classroom and sat on a bench all alone.

After a few minutes, I returned to the hostel. That day, the same college, which I had loved a lot, felt like a graveyard. I walked back to the hostel alone. I was the only one back as the others were still in college. I opened my room and went inside, kept my bag on my bed and sat in a corner.

There was silence everywhere, except for the sound of the vehicles crossing the hostel building.

As soon as we met, I knew you were the one
The one I would spend my days thinking of
And the one I would spend my nights dreaming about
The one who would hold me when I cried
And the one who would laugh with me
The one who I would share my life with
And the one I would love
I knew all that as soon as we met.

My heartbeat stopped, thinking of those words for her. She was going far from me. I burst into tears. The tears burst forth like water from a dam, spilling down my face. I felt like a distressed child, raw from the inside. It took something out of me. She had stolen my spirit; an injury no other person could see.

I kept on crying loudly; my tears were not stopping that day. I pushed my face into my pillow and kept crying. I don't remember when I fell asleep, crying, but I woke up hearing the voices of my hostel mates, asking me to come down for dinner.

"Is everything fine?" Akash asked me while I had my dinner. I nodded, saying all was well. But he had more questions, "You were back early today."

"Yes, I was not feeling well," I replied. Akash did not ask anything more but his silence had many questions, for which I did not have answers.

I remained seated in the mess, even after everyone left. She had stopped talking and had muted my whole life. I lost interest in friends, life or family. My mind was only thinking about her.

I knew what I was going through, but I didn't want to share it with my friends.

I wasn't sure what I should do. If I forced her, maybe I'd hurt her more, or should I leave it to time and wait for her to come back to me? I was in a dilemma.

Since the last three days, I was going to college and was sitting outside the classroom, watching her in pain from outside. She did not even bother to look at me. If I stopped to dwell on her for even a fraction of a second, my face became wet with tears. I know she loved me, but I couldn't reach her thoughts. It was cruel that the sun continued to rise, to welcome each new day devoid of her laughter or even her grumpy complaints and loveable commentary. I wanted to hear her voice calling me stupid or her trying to make me touch her hand and blame it on her feet. I wanted her to leave her handkerchief on the floor and forget to take it along, and wait for lunch and to have tiffin with me.

By then, everyone knew that something had happened between both of us. But I was not worried about it. I was not worried about anything then. I was not worried about my studies; I was not concerned about food; I was not concerned about my health; I was not worried about my family; I was not concerned about anything else apart from her.

She was behaving differently; she was not looking at me and she had stopped smiling. She avoided everyone and she was grave and sullen.

I decided to talk to her and would not leave without getting my answers. I sat outside the class and waited for it to get over. After some time, the professor left and the students came out.

I was looking shabby. My hair had grown long, I was badly dressed with an unshaven beard. After some time, she came out, along with Chaaru and Reena, holding her books in her hands. She kept talking to Chaaru, ignoring me. For me, everything was still. I could see no one else on the campus and I could not see what others might have been thinking. I didn't give a damn.

I stood up from the bench on which I was sitting and followed her. I ignored all 'hellos' in between and moved straight behind her. She was walking towards the main gate along with her friends. I kept following her; she parted from them and began walking alone. An excellent opportunity to talk to her. I took long steps and reached her. I called her name from behind. She turned, looked and kept walking. I pulled her right hand, holding her from the elbow and came in front of her. She stopped and avoided eye contact.

"I need to talk to you." I came straight to the point. She kept staring at me in anger and then without speaking a word tried to leave. I again tried to obstruct her way and in a loud voice said, "You need to talk to me, Vaidehi."

But she did not say a single word and kept walking. This time I didn't stop her, as I didn't want to create a scene. She moved, while I stood there with my hands on my waist.

"If you want to forget someone, never hate him. Everything and everyone that you hate gets engraved upon your heart; if you want to let go of something, if you want to forget, you cannot hate!" I shouted from behind.

She heard me as her steps slowed down. I continued, "I know you love me. If we can talk, we can sort it out."

She continued walking without turning back. I stood at the same place at the corner of the main gate and shouted again,

"Vaidehi, I love you, and remember, I will not move an inch from here if you won't talk to me."

She stopped, listening to my last words. I felt a ray of hope thinking she would come and talk, but then she turned to me to give me a grave look, and moved on.

"I am not joking. I will not be moving from this place. I will stand here till my last breath!" I shouted, but she walked on, taking long steps.

I kept standing there, looking at her till she disappeared from my eyes. I could see students now moving out from college. Some of them waved at me by leaning on their bikes and scooters. But I kept standing there, waiting for her to come back. I was feeling thirsty, but I had promised, I would not move an inch, and so, there I was. I was sure I'd die for her if she would not come back to me.

She walked off and the gap she left behind just can't be filled by anyone else. She had got engraved in my DNA. I know she stopped talking because of some fault of mine, but I was struggling to know what it was. Now that she wasn't here to hold my hand, I stood all alone and had no courage to act. But she would always be my girlfriend, even though she was my mute girlfriend now.

I stood there, with my eyes wet and heart dull, with hope in my heart that she would come back. After some time, Anurag and Akash came out from the campus gate and saw me standing there all alone. They were still not aware of what had happened between Vaidehi and me, but they could smell the fumes.

"Hey Rohan, waiting for someone? Come, let's go to the hostel, Anurag will drop us there," Akash asked me sitting on the back seat of Anurag' scooter. I didn't know what to reply, but I was adamant that I wouldn't move from there.

"You carry on. I am waiting for someone," I replied.

"Okay then bye, will see you in the hostel," he replied, while Thakur drove his scooter to the left side of the road.

As they went off, I turned my wrist to check the time; it was three. It was a hot afternoon, with bright sun on my back, but the heat was less scorching than the burning of my heart. I looked around and found a big stone kept on the side. I sat on it, facing the road.

With doubt in my heart, I was sure she would come back, but already one hour had passed, and she hadn't returned. By that time, most of the students had left for the day, and I was all alone waiting at the corner of the lonely road of Jabalpur Cantonment. I picked up a small stick, which was lying there and wondered what could have happened.

Before leaving for my semester break of the second semester, I remembered I got the annual function pictures printed, which I had clicked using a new camera and had brought them to show her. She was excited to see the snaps as she had performed superbly and was looking exquisite that day. While she was looking through the album, she asked me something and I hadn't had an answer to at that moment.

She suddenly noticed that most of the snaps in the album were hers in various performances and poses. I had already asked Anurag and he said he had taken her pictures as he felt he must take as many photos of his bhabhi for me as he could.

"Out of the two hundred and fifty pictures taken, how come two hundred are mine?" Vaidehi asked me suspiciously.

I had no answer to it and replied, "It's just a coincidence. Maybe because you took part in maximum shows."

"But most are of me alone. Who clicked them?" she further questioned.

I tried to take it lightly and replied, "I remembered Anurag did, but it's not intentional." I tried to assure her.

She kept looking at me with suspicious eyes and then said, "Hope you are saying the truth Rohan, because if I come to know that you have told everyone in your hostel about us, to make fun of, that day will be the last when you would hear your name from my mouth."

She looked serious when she warned me, but I didn't pay heed.

But can this be the reason for her not speaking or was it something else?

It was six in the evening. The sun has already set when I saw Akash and Vineet on a bike, coming towards me.

As they reached close to me, Vineet parked the bike.

"Wow! A Yamaha Rx100!" I asked them to divert their minds.

But in vain. They understood that there was something going on. They got down from the bike and sat next to me. After a few seconds, Akash asked, "Will you tell us, or must we start beating you?"

I said after a pause, "She has stopped talking to me suddenly."

"And you are sitting here, waiting for her, hoping that she will come running to you to talk, like in the movies," Vineet interrupted with a chagrined expression.

I smiled wistfully.

"C'mon, get up and let's go back to the hostel," he said holding my hand and pulling me up.

I resisted, "Bhai, please, I believe she will come to meet me; she can't see me sitting here all alone."

"Are you a fool or what, Rohan? You know her attitude. She never even talked to her batch-mates and you believe that she will come to console you?" Akash shouted at me.

"My heart says she will come," I replied softly with confidence and continued. "At least let me try. You don't want us to get together again?"

"Whom you are fooling Rohan? She was never with you. She needed a toy to play with in the first year of college, and she used you."

"This is not the case," I retorted.

"You know this, and if this is not the case, why has she stopped talking to you for no reason? I have seen many break-ups but a break-up without reason, I have seen for the first time in my life," Vineet said raising his voice.

Hearing them made me more adamant. "Whatever, I will not be leaving this place," I reiterated.

"And what about the warden or if your parents call?" Akash asked

I looked at him with pleading eyes, "I need your help. Take care of the warden and if anyone calls from home, tell them I am not in the hostel."

Vineet was really concerned for me; he asked Akash to bring a bottle of water and give it to me. Akash went inside the college campus to fill a water bottle. Vineet sat on his haunches, holding my hands and said, "I know you love her and if she loves you, I believe she will come, but promise if she doesn't turn by midnight, you will come back with us to the hostel."

I could see a true friend in his eyes.

I smiled and assured him. Meanwhile, Akash came running with the water. They handed over the bottle and sat on the bike.

"What if she never comes?" I asked Vineet as they were about to leave.

Vineet kept looking into my eyes and moved on, leaving me behind. If there was confusion in any relationship, people talk, fight to resolve, but she was behaving differently, confusing me. I couldn't understand how to handle her.

My mind was puzzled remembering her touch, her kisses, her smile. Having heard of strangers becoming friends, now friends becoming strangers was annoying me.

I kept on looking at my watch, and every ticking of its hand seemed like a year. Darkness took over, and bugs started disturbing me. I was feeling hungry and drowned. My energy level was going down, and my eyes were closing. I kept on remembering those beautiful moments spent with her and tried to keep my energy level up. But somewhere in my heart, I had lost hope.

She had turned every moment we had spent together into painful memories. They were sharp and cut right through me every time I thought about them. She turned me into this broken mess, and even if I wouldn't hear her again, her touch would be with me for years, or maybe for the rest of my life.

At a distance, I saw a bike coming towards me. In the brightness of the street light, I saw Vineet along with Akash rushing towards me. My energy was spent. My eyes became wet when they reached me, and before even they could say anything to me, I burst into tears. Tears flowed down my cheeks.

Salty drops fell from my chin, drenching my shirt. Perhaps these tears would help wash the pain. I pressed my head against Vineet's shoulder and I couldn't stop crying. The wound was fresh. It was raw. And my friends were letting me cry. They knew crying would make my heart light. They knew I was in pain. I cried and fainted on his shoulder.

I know I had a girlfriend, but my mute girlfriend was hurting me a lot.

Vineet

I *am a person who believes in lust, and there was no place of love for me, but holding Rohan that night, I could feel the pain of love. Even I wanted someone who could love me like Rohan loved Vaidehi. He taught me that love is far superior to lust and what is the true meaning of love. He made me understand the real meaning of the words 'I love you'. That means I would defend you with my life, whatever may happen. It means I will comfort you during trying times. It means I will dance and rejoice with you when times are good. It means I will never betray you, never give up on you. Love says I will forgive you when you make a mistake. Love says I will never abandon you. It means I will never put you in danger.*

He cried like a baby in my arms, and I let him. I wanted him to shed all his pain that night. He cried, and I kept holding him. And then he fainted. Akash suggested to give him some water, but I stopped him because I knew it would be tough to take him back if he woke up again.

We picked him and placed him on our bike. Akash kept holding him from behind and we took him back to the hostel. His body was burning with fever; we made him sleep in his room and watched over him the entire night. He kept on recalling her name in pain, over and over again.

I was concerned about my friend and was angry with Vaidehi. I had always doubted her; her attitude had made me sceptical. Many people have break-ups, but they have just reasons.

Also, I would not only blame her, but Rohan was also a fool who had left Navya whom he had loved for so many years for a girl who never wanted to be his. I saw Navya during his sister's marriage; she was damn beautiful and her eyes expressed how much she loved him. But my friend Rohan was mad about Vaidehi and blinded by her.

According to me, her attitude was the cause of her weird behaviour. We had got our second-semester results, and Vaidehi had topped again. Maybe she felt ashamed to have Rohan as her friend who passed with a mediocre percentage. She was an ambitious girl, and she dreamt about Mercedes cars and bungalows. Maybe after her visit to Rohan's house, she understood that her dreams could not be fulfilled with him, so she wanted to move on.

But, I am only concerned about my friend and nothing else. Sometimes I also feel, maybe Vaidehi didn't know how to deal with boys, as she had studied in a girl's school. She might need to understand her approach towards boys. Maybe her way of interaction or dealing with boys was not correct.

But I feel, individually Rohan and Vaidehi both are great human beings, but they were not made for each other. And the sooner Rohan can understand this, it would be better for him.

I know it would be tough for Rohan to forget her memories, but it's only he who can help himself in such a situation. We as friends can only support him.

Present day
Dehradun

I reached my hotel in Dehradun on Rajpura Road at midnight. I informed Rajesh, my driver that we would leave for Meerut in the morning, so he could rest.

The company had booked rooms in a hotel for the employees to stay in. This was one of the best facilities which Hutch HR provided us. I was never tense about not getting a hotel room or paying for one.

I reached the reception and presented my employee identity card; he immediately handed over my room keys. I entered my room, which was plush. I put my luggage down and removed my shoes. I picked up an ashtray which was kept on the centre table, and made myself comfortable on the bed.

I pulled out a cigarette and smoked while thinking of how to contact her. My mobile was damaged and so I couldn't see her number and message. After taking a few puffs, my mind started working. I worked in a telecom company, so getting data out of any user was simple for me.

I picked up the land phone of the hotel and dialled the main switching centre of Hutch in Meerut. The main switching centre was on the first floor in the same office where I used to work, so most of the employees who worked there knew me.

In telecom, whatever we do in our mobiles is saved in the switching centre. Governing bodies use this data to trace criminals. I dialled the switching centre number.

"Hello, this is Kamal, who's this?"

Thank god it was Kamal who picked up the phone. He was the switching centre in-charge and a great friend of mine.

"Hi Kamal, it's Rohan."

"From which number are you calling and where is your mobile? Mahajan Sir was trying to contact you," he informed me.

Mahajan Sir was my boss. He was the most intelligent and calm person I had ever met in my life. Supportive to his subordinates and an excellent example of a perfect boss.

I informed Kamal about my mobile, which had gotten damaged.

"How can I get a new SIM with the same number and my data?" I asked him.

He thought for a while and then gave me the solution, "Tomorrow morning, you can visit our distribution point in Dehradun and collect a SIM and tell me its registration number. I will configure the same number on it."

"And what about my data in that SIM?" I asked with curiosity as that was more important for me.

"That's lost in your old SIM," he confirmed.

"Numbers I am fine, I can collect them, but I need your help," I urged him

"What?"

"I received a message before it got damaged and I need that number urgently. My friend, I know you can get that for me," I pleaded

He thought for a while and then replied, "What if Mahajan Sir comes to know, that I took out data for you."

I finally begged and requested him, "Please... please... please."

"Okay... okay... call me in some time and I will pull that number and will let you know," he replied.

I thanked him again and again and then disconnected the call. I thanked god for making me an employee in the telecom industry.

I pulled out the second cigarette and started smoking. Every second felt like a year to me. I wanted her number and wanted to call her. I would hear her voice after five long years.

After a few minutes, Kamal called me back. "What is the number of the last messages I received at approximately six p.m.?" I asked.

He asked me to wait, till he checked the same and then gave me her number. I immediately noted it down on a notepad.

"Thanks Kamal, you saved my life," I thanked him.

It was 1:15 a.m. Should I call her now or must I wait till morning? I was confused, but my soul urged me to go ahead and hear her voice. I picked up the receiver of the phone and gasped.

My heartbeat was racing. I dialled her number, holding my breath.

"*The mobile number you are trying to reach is either switched off or out of coverage area,*" the prerecorded voice announced.

I tried again only to hear the same recorded voice. I tried again and again and got frustrated. Maybe her mobile was switched off.

I was feeling frustrated as I did not have her landline number.

I got out of the bed and opened my laptop bag. I wanted to find Vineet's number in my Yahoo mailbox. As I remembered he added his number below his signature in his emails. I switched on my laptop and lit one more cigarette. As I blew the smoke on my laptop, I could recall how broken I was after Vineet brought me to the hostel that night.

▼

I had high fever the next day, and my friends asked me to stay in the hostel while they went to college. I lay in my hostel bed, with long hair and beard and swollen eyes, wrapped in a quilt. I opened my eyes and felt the silence in the hostel. The window of my room was half open, from which sunlight was peeping in. I lay straight and watched the rotating fan above me. I kept looking at it. *Why can't I end my life?*

I kept on thinking, depressed. But the faces of my mom, dad, sister, and Vaidehi gave me strength. No, I could not commit suicide as I had promised to Vaidehi, that no matter what, I would never think of ending my life, and she had also promised that no matter what, she would always love me. I was confident she still did; it was just a matter of time before this was sorted.

Though I was still feeling feverish, I put on my jeans and t-shirt and opened the door to go to college. Sitting alone in the hostel was making me feel worse. I went out and hailed a rickshaw. I was not carrying my books or bag, as I was sure I would not attend any classes. I could not think about anything else except Vaidehi.

As I reached college, I went in and took a seat outside my class. I could see her sitting inside the class and concentrating on the lecture going on. My eyes were fixed on her unblinking. After sometimes, she turned and saw me sitting and gave me a grave look. I didn't flinch and kept staring at her.

I had already missed ten days' classes by then.

I was sitting in the sun when Reena came from behind as I was lost in my thoughts.

"Will this affect her?" she asked placing her hand on my shoulder from behind.

I turned and looked at her with no expression and replied softly, "You are not attending the lecture?"

She moved to the front and took a seat next to me on the same bench on which I was sitting and replied, "No, I was not interested today. But what happened to you? Look at yourself."

I know how I was looking and didn't reply.

"You boarded the wrong bus, Rohan; that's the reason you have landed at the wrong destination."

She tried to explain to me. I would not blame her for what she was explaining, as that was what she knew about us. I kept silent and after sometime she stood up, as I was not showing any interest in talking to her.

As she stood up, I asked her, "Can you help me, Reena?" she heard me and sat down. "Yes, I have been observing you. I don't want you to lose hope, Rohan. Tell me, how can I help you?"

"Can you talk to her on my behalf?" I asked her and continued. "She is not talking to me, I don't know why, can you help me to patch up with her."

"No way. You know her better than me. She will not entertain me at all." But I pleaded with her and, finally, she agreed.

"Let me talk to her once she is out."

Meanwhile, she tried to counsel me a lot, and I kept nodding without listening. I had not known that she was so concerned about me. "Do you not have any other friend as I have not seen you with anyone else since your break-up?"

I looked at her in surprise. "Please Reena, don't call it a break-up. It's just a misunderstanding between us."

She smiled and then we saw that class had got over.

"Vaidehi is coming out, can you please talk to her?" I again pleaded with her.

"Wait, let me speak to her," she replied and went to her. I kept sitting in the same place and observed her approaching Vaidehi.

Vineet and Anurag saw me sitting and rushed towards me.

"Why did you come to college?" Vineet touched my forehead. I was still feverish. "You will die, man, stand up! Let me drop you back to the hostel."

Vineet was speaking to me while I sat without responding. I wanted to know the outcome of Reena' s conversation with Vaidehi. I could see Reena explaining something to her and she was giving a sullen look. Vaidehi was saying something to her, while her hand movement showed that she was not interested in talking about me.

After five minutes, Reena returned. I stood up and walked towards her, leaving behind Vineet and Anurag.

"What did she say? Did she agree to talk to me?"

Reena grimaced. "I am sorry Rohan, she is adamant. She told me that if I want to be your advocate, she'll not speak to me either."

Her attitude was getting to me. I left Reena and walked towards Vaidehi in anger. I wanted clarification.

I went up to her as she stood with Chaaru. I stood in front of her, with an angry expression on my face. She looked directly into my eyes, sardonically. I went to speak out to her. I went to hurt her with my words. I went to say she was wrong. I went to say she was doing wrong to me. I went to say I miss her. I went to cry. I went to plead. But I stood in front of her, looking into her eyes, frozen. She stood in front of me, unblinking, and so did I. Time stopped moving. I refused to look away, even as my lips trembled and my shoulders heaved with emotion, unwilling to back down. My dark lashes brimmed heavy with tears; my hands clenched into shaking fists in a desperate battle against her muteness.

But her eyes stopped me from getting harsh, her lips stopped me from shouting, her breath stopped me from speaking.

A lone tear traced down my cheek, and just like that, the floodgates opened.

I wept, tears streaming from my eyes. Loud, heaving sobs tearing from my throat, and still, I did not look away. She continued watching me without pain. I could not speak a word. That day I realized, I had lost her forever. I had lost her smile. I had lost her friendship. I had lost my comfort. I had lost her voice, but still somewhere in my heart, I believed she was my girlfriend – my mute girlfriend.

She kept watching me and then left without wiping my tears. I must not have cried to prove the strong man inside, but her eyes made me realize that I had lost her forever in this life.

I accepted that she would not talk to me. Four months passed, and still, my eyes were burning, and my chest felt heavy. I could no longer see clearly. All I knew was that she was gone, out of my life for possibly forever. Alone on the terrace of my hostel, I stood up and remembered my loneliness.

I was broken and kept to myself. I hardly smiled, did not have any kind of fun, nor chatted with my friends. I sat on the terrace or in my room all alone, thinking about her. In the third semester, I had not attended a single lecture, nor had I purchased any books. But I never missed a single day of college. I went every day and sat on the bench outside our class, watching her. I wanted her to realize that I was nothing without her. I rarely talked to my parents now by myself, and only attended the calls when they did.

I was sitting all alone when Anna came to the terrace, "Hey Rohan, what are you doing alone here?" he asked me and came next to me.

I smiled at him casually, and kept looking at the road where once Vaidehi stood chatting with me. Anna took out a cigarette and lit it to smoke. As he blew smoke from his mouth, it came towards me. I had found something to forget her.

"Can I take one cigarette?" I asked Anna looking at him.

"But you don't smoke," Anna replied.

"I am burning all over, only that the smoke was not visible. Let that come out from me," I expressed my wish.

"It's Wills Flake, a pretty strong cigarette."

I picked up his packet, which he placed on the table where we were sitting and pulled out one cigarette.

"Are you sure?" he again asked me wide-eyed.

I was sure; I wanted to smoke. I placed the cigarette on my lips and lit it. And then I took a puff, sucked deep to take it till the last point in the chest. I coughed and coughed loudly. Anna pressed my back as tears flowed from my eyes, but I wanted to take the next puff.

I pushed Anna's hand away and took another puff and then blew smoke from my mouth. Something strange moved in my mind. I knew I was doing something wrong, but I loved all the things now which could make my life miserable.

"Exam dates are out. Sessionals are starting from next week followed by exams of the third semester. Are you prepared?" Anna asked me. That was news for me as I hadn't attended any class in the last four months.

I gave a sly smile and took more puffs and kept looking in front, with no tension of studies or exams.

"May I take one more cigarette?"

"Sure, but don't smoke too much," Anna replied. A friend who was a chain smoker was concerned about me. What irony! "Okay, I am going to my room. I need to study for the first sessional for Mechanics," he informed me and left taking his packet of cigarettes while I kept sitting there, thinking about Mechanics. *Is this a subject we have in this semester?*

I was not even aware of my subjects of the third semester, but I was not concerned about it. I was only concerned about hearing her voice.

I kept walking around the hostel all alone. I pushed myself into my room and kept my door closed, as if I could trap the memories inside. But once I opened it, every recollection would race towards me like a slap in the face, drenching me in intense sadness.

Though my hostel mates tried to be there for me, the truth was, that I was all alone.

I was sitting in my room on my bed with cigarette in my mouth, leaning on the pillow, with no sound or movement, while Akash was sitting on the other side, busy preparing for the Mechanics sessional.

"Why don't you prepare for the sessional?" Akash asked me showing his concern. I didn't reply, busy trying to make rings from the cigarette smoke.

"I am speaking to you Rohan. That girl has spoiled your life. Forget her, think about your career and stop smoking."

I looked him and smiled. "She loved me. It's me who wants to get destroyed."

"You will gain nothing by doing this. You are wasting your own life and time," he tried to convince me.

"This time is the biggest problem, my friend. I am trying to move on, but fucking time is not budging. It's stuck with her memories. My life was worth it because of her; if she is not there, what is the use of this fucking life!" I retorted with a glazed look.

"Rohan, four months have passed. Friend, come out of this, I care for you," he reiterated, showing concern.

I stood up, picked up my cigarette packet and went out saying, "Sorry for disturbing you friend; you study. I will waste my time downstairs."

"Wait Rohan, listen to me…." he shouted from behind, but I would not stop.

The whole night I sat on the sofa in the lobby area. I went up to my room to sleep at five in the morning. I knew I was spoiling my career, but my mind and heart were not listening.

These feelings I had for her couldn't vanish until my body ceased to function and my soul got released. My mind wanted to save me from sinking, but my heart was pushing me down. I still believed however deep I'd fall, she'd be there to hold me.

On the first sessional day, I dressed up and reached college. With no energy and no interest in the sessional as I had not even touched my books, I just went for the heck of it.

My eyes were red and there was a cigarette on my lips when I reached college along with Akash and Vineet. I threw my cigarette before entering the campus.

I was worried as I had not studied at all. Worried not about failing, but afraid of how ashamed I'd be in front of my friends and Vaidehi.

As we moved inside, our batch-mates were gathered in the open quadrangle area, sitting on stairs and side elevated floor, books in their hands, discussing, remembering and recalling. I observed them and listened to their discussions, then went to the corner and sat alone. I did not have books or notes with me. My mind was blacked out. People had studied a lot, and they were expecting a tough viva inside.

As my eyes wandered, I saw Vaidehi sitting in front of the room, where the viva was going on, with Mechanics book on her lap murmuring. I remembered the first and the second semester sessional when I was sitting next to her and we both were laughing and enjoying our studies. But time had changed everything. I tried to concentrate on the conversations others were having on Mechanics. I knew I was blank, but maybe something which I would hear would help.

It was a hot summer day. I could feel sweat flowing down my head, I tried to wipe my forehead with my sleeves. Vaidehi looked at me. I could see her handkerchief in her hand, but she didn't offer it that day. She continued studying, and I continued my observation.

The first batch of five students, which included Anurag, came out of the room after half an hour. Everyone rushed to them to know what questions were asked. Anurag looked unhappy. I stood up and went to him.

"Bhai, external is mad inside; the heat wave has entered his head this summer," Anurag was explaining in his style.

"But what happened, what he was asking?" someone questioned him among the mob of frustrated engineers.

"He is asking tough questions from Mechanics, like different type of forces, law of parallelogram, State Varignons theorem, etc." Hearing him, some intelligent people smiled and some who had not studied, moved aside turning the pages of their books to have a quick look at those questions.

I had not even heard those words in the last six months. It sounded like Greek to me.

Getting tensed looking at everyone, my head ached. I was feeling depressed, dull and deprived of energy. I walked to the back of the building where there was a drinking water tap.

I washed my face, drank some water and moved to the side and stood in the shade of a big Banyan tree. I pulled out a cigarette and lit it, looking around to see if there was a teacher. I wiped my face with my sleeves and took a puff when I saw Vaidehi along with Chaaru walking to the tap.

She looked at me indifferently. I knew she didn't like me smoking, but I was smoking only because of her, and I wanted her to see that. I wanted her to feel my pain; I wanted her to think about me.

She continued drinking water, and I kept smoking, looking at her. Chaaru smiled at me and I smiled back. They left after drinking water, while I kept watching her from a distance.

I kept smoking when I saw Vaidehi's handkerchief on the corner of the elevated wall. I threw the cigarette I was smoking, and went to pick it up. Did she leave it for me or did she forget it? I was not sure, but I took it and went to the other side of the building where she was standing.

"Please give this handkerchief to Vaidehi," I said passing it Chaaru.

Chaaru took it from my hand while Vaidehi looked at me unblinking. Chaaru gave the handkerchief to her, and she took it and moved her eyes back to her book.

As I turned and walked back, I saw another batch coming out. They looked worried as well. Suddenly my throat went dry; I could feel my heart beating fast. I was sweating and my head was heavy. I looked at the sky and felt dizzy. And that was the last thing I remember.

I had fainted and fallen to the ground. My classmates who were standing next to me immediately pulled me and took me to the shade, made me sit comfortably on a chair and loosened my shirt buttons. I could remember Anurag running with water and splashing it on my face and then someone giving me a glass of glucose. Everyone gathered around me and among all those faces, one face was the most tense, which I could remember, and that was Vaidehi's – my mute girlfriend who was standing in front of me. Someone was wiping my face, and I could smell the fragrance of her handkerchief.

After some time, I felt relaxed and opened my eyes. Vineet and Anurag asked me to stay calm and keep sitting there, till my turn came for the sessional. I nodded and sat silently, moving my head back. I could still see her standing at some distance, in front of me, looking concerned. Her wet handkerchief was lying next to me .

I wanted to say, "I know you love me, your handkerchief lying next to me is proof. You looked concerned for me, which is an energy-booster for me. I can feel your love even when you are not speaking to me. I can feel your presence even when you are not near me. I know you feel the same, but my mind is blank as I fail to understand your muteness."

"Get up Rohan; it's your turn now for the sessional. All the best."

Anurag helped me to get up and took me to the door.

I thanked him and entered the sessional room, along with Vaidehi and three more batch-mates. We sat on five chairs, in front of the big table. The external and our internal teacher sat in front of us. There were papers and a register in front of them, in which our names were written.

The fan above was trying its best to give us cool air, which I needed desperately.

Our internal professor took attendance first, and when he called my name, he looked at me through his spectacles and asked sarcastically: "Are you a new student? Seeing you for the first time."

I was depressed and looked down. He continued and asked the first question.

"What are boilers?"

Tensed as I did not know its answer, Vaidehi started it and completed it in one go. The external professor appreciated her and asked the second question to Vedanta sitting next to me, "What are the classifications of the force system?"

Vedanta, who was average in studies and was far behind me in the last year two semesters, explained it. I was more nervous hearing his explanation as I did not know any answers.

The external moved his eyes on me, as I tried to look down, avoiding eye contact with him. "Type of boilers, can you answer that?" he asked me.

I became dumb. The fact that there were different boilers was also a surprise. I looked at the ceiling roof and tried to pretend I knew but wasn't able to recall. He kept watching me and then I looked down at Vaidehi' s hands. She was carrying a paper which she was hiding under the table; I could look at it without the professors noticing.

Without looking at me, she wrote something on the paper, 'WATER TUBE AND FIRE TUBE'

I understood, she was trying to help me, and I started reading it. It was not so clear but I tried to read it, pretending as if I was trying to recall the answer. "Water, fire tube," I spoke softly.

"Okay," the external replied, but was not convinced. He asked me the second question, "What are manholes in boilers?"

I didn't know what to say. I leaned to see if Vaidehi was writing something. I could see she was trying to, but it was not a one-word answer. I wiped my forehead.

"You don't know about manholes? Why are you looking here and there? Who would say you are here to be an engineer? Don't waste your parents' money," the professor scolded me. I looked down. My friends sitting next to me looked worried as the external was angry and he'd take their class as well.

Just then, Vaidehi interrupted him, "Sir, he's outstanding in studies. Just before the sessional, he fainted because of the heat. He has high fever as well."

I looked at her unblinking. She cared for me; I had heard her voice after a long time. Her voice flooded me with energy.

"Thanks for informing us, Vaidehi. Rohan, you could have told us this. Please get up and send the next batch. Get some rest, Rohan."

I thanked him, and we all moved out. As we moved out of the room, I came close to her and spoke: "Thank you Vaidehi." But she didn't reply and walked off with Chaaru. I kept standing there confused. What did she want? Why was she doing this to me?

I looked around and tried to find Vineet. I needed to discuss what had happened inside. I rushed to him, holding his shoulder and pulled him to the corner.

"What happened Rohan? How was your viva?"

I took him alone and narrated everything that had happened inside. I asked him his opinion on her behaviour.

He thought for a while after listening to me replied, "Rohan, what I feel is that she likes you, she cares for you as a human being and as she is wonderful by heart, she helped you. Maybe if someone else would have been there, she would have done the same. This doesn't mean she loves you. And about her not talking to you, she is ambitious and has an attitude. She would never go out with a boy average in everything. She knows she is intelligent; she is the college topper, and she is beautiful, no doubt about that. She can choose the best out of the best in future. Try to understand Rohan, forget her, she can never be your partner. She was with you as a friend, and when she realized you thought she was more than that, she took a step back and this is the truth."

He explained in clear words, but he was wrong. He didn't know about our conversations in the last one year; about how many times we kissed, and what we had planned for our future. I could not let her go.

While we were talking, I saw her walking out of the main gate on her scooty. I wanted to talk to her. I wanted an answer to why she had helped me if she didn't love me. I shouted her name and ran towards her, pushing Vineet aside. He tried to stop me, but I would not stop. My shirt buttons tore while he tried to pull me, but I ran behind her. She could not hear me, but I shouted her name, like a mad man. Vineet followed me. I wiped the sweat from my forehead, exhausted. My long legs broke beneath me. My heart raced, but I knew I had to keep going. I kept on shouting her name, while she raced on her bike. Vineet ran towards me faster to hold me, leaving behind his bag and books. I was losing my breath when Vineet caught my shirt from behind. He pulled me, making me slip on the hot tarred road. I fell on the road. I pushed him and pulled myself up to run behind her. I was bleeding from cuts and bruises. Vineet too got up, and before I ran again, he pulled me back and slapped me hard.

"Motu... she is going Motu, I need to talk to her... let me go," I shouted and cried. Vineet stopped me. He hugged me tightly and tried to calm me down.

"Rohan, stop. She is going home, not going from your life. You can talk to her later," he consoled me. I cried, down on my knees. Vineet hugged me and wiped my tears. I wanted to hear her voice. I sobbed into his chest unceasingly, hands clutching at his jacket.

She had gone away again, without speaking a word and I stood with a cigarette in my mouth, smoking and recalling my girlfriend who was now a mute girlfriend.

I was lost in her memories and would remain locked in my room in the hostel. Cigarettes were my best friends and my roommate Akash preferred to study in a different room, than watch my morose face. There were three days left for the first exam of the third semester which was Mathematics and I had not even purchased the books yet. I didn't give a damn. I wanted to show her my defeat; I wanted to show her my pain.

Someone knocked on the door, while I was busy brooding. The door opened. It was Neeraj sir, my senior from Delhi. He came in and closed the door. He was holding a cigarette. He took a puff and came to me. I smiled at him and wished him a good evening.

He was the only senior who had never ragged us. He came and sat in front of me on the chair while I remained on the bed. He kept looking at me unblinking. I was not aware what he was up to. Then he threw away his cigarette and asked me, "What is your name?"

I smiled, "Sir you know, I am Rohan..." He gave me a tight slap. I was shocked as the ragging period was already over, and he had been out of it all. The slap was so hard, it shook my head and soul.

He asked again, "What is your name?"

This time I replied, "My name is Rohan Verma." Again he slapped me. This time it was much harder. Before he questioned me further, I recalled the rules of ragging "Sir, my name is Rohan Verma sir."

He leaned back, kept looking at me. "It hurts, Rohan?" I looked at him and nodded. He continued.

"It's not hurting physically; you have received harder slaps than this. This hurts because you had not expected me to hit you."

My first teardrop made its way down my cheek as he continued, "You are in pain because you did not expect Vaidehi to ditch you. Similarly, you would be hurting her, if she had not expected this from you. And failing in your exam will hurt your parents as they will not have expected this from you. It hurts Rohan when someone does something not expected from him.

"What are you thinking? That you will get her back by these emotional dramas? Forget her Rohan, forget her forever.

"She is an ambitious and intelligent girl. She would never love a boy defeated by his own emotions. No girl will ever like to be with a boy who cannot even take care of himself. How can she trust you?" he continued and I kept listening to him.

"One thing I've learned about humans is that you can't judge their strength by the size of their actions, but by the devotion of an act, no matter how small. You tell me, what devotion she would see in you now?"

I was silent. His slaps had cleared my brain.

"I know she loved you, and I am sure she loves you because girls are not like boys; if they love someone, they love with their soul, and as far as I know her, she is a girl with the best soul, and she can never ditch you. But yes, the way you are behaving in front of her would make her wonder whether she was correct.

"I don't know her so closely, but people say she is full of attitude and if it is such a case, get to the bottom of her attitude. Analyze why she should have an attitude or be proud? Because she is beautiful? You too are handsome. Because she is charming?

You too were. Because she is intelligent? You too are. Because she is a college topper? Yes, here you miss out! So only one reason for her to leave you? Rohan, be a man, don't give up!

"You tried reaching her by every means in the last six months, but you failed. Try another way. Show her who you are. Remember she became attracted to you because of who you were when you joined college. Now she can't find the same Rohan in you. If she is showing attitude, show her the same mirror back.

"I will suggest if you want her back, bring that energetic and innovative Rohan back, make that Rohan more vibrant and colourful. Make him so gorgeous, that she can't stop herself from reaching him. Make him so intelligent, that she learns from him. And the day you do that, I can promise you, she will be back with you. Remember, the best proof of love is trust, so don't screw her trust in you; your love will last forever."

His words reached my heart and mind. His slaps had worked. Some positive energy flowed into my body. It felt like I had found new hope to live for. I had found a new way to win her back. My smile was back on my face.

I stood from my bed and hugged him, with tears in my eyes. He too hugged me like I was his baby.

"Sir, I promise you, you will not find me sitting alone in the future. From now onwards, my goal will be to get her back, but not with a negative approach," I replied with energy, wiping my tears.

He smiled and gestured. "Rohan, three days left for the first exam. Prove yourself. She will expect you to fail in the exam in this semester. Prove her wrong. Show her that the real Rohan is back," he emphasized.

"My body felt like a cage, and you have unlocked me with your words. Opened a door I didn't know was there. You took out the pain and made it bearable by still seeing the person I truly am. And for that reason alone, I feel I will be a bird in the sky again, able to sing once more," I said and thanked him.

I thanked him again and again for his motivation. Now it was my turn to prove myself. I need to plan my preparation and show everyone that Rohan Verma was back.

As he left, I went to the washroom. I looked at my face in the mirror. Dishevelled and shabby. This wasn't the real me. I poured some foam in my hand and applied it on my face. I pulled out a razor which had been lying unused for months. I shaved my beard. With every move of the blade on my face, I could see a new energetic Rohan coming out.

"*Vaidehi, you have seen two Rohans till now. The third one will emerge now. More energetic, fun and friendly.*"

I washed my face; a new Rohan was born.

I changed into fresh clothes and moved downstairs to the STD booth. Most of my friends were in their rooms preparing for the mathematics exam.

I entered the STD booth and dialled Anurag's home. As he picked up I said, "Anurag, *kameene, bhool gaya kya mujhe?*"

"Hey, Rohan! You're sounding happy after a long time," he replied.

"I need your help. Can you come to the hostel now?" I asked, without wasting time.

He thought for a second and then agreed. I waited downstairs for him.

As I saw him coming on his scooter, I ran to him and hugged him as he stopped. "Oh! Wow, my Rohan is back!" he said happily.

I smiled back and asked, "Can you take me to Hanuman Taal? I need to buy the books of the third semester."

Anurag immediately agreed and asked me to sit behind him on his scooter.

A real friend is one who walks in when the rest of the world walks out.

Anurag was one of them.

After we had bought the books, he dropped me back to the hostel. I was still not sure how I'd cover the syllabus in three days, but I was confident.

I leaned back on my chair in my room and thought with closed eyes. *How must I begin?*

There is no time left for me to practice sums one by one. I must read them.

This was the solution. It was better to keep reading the book and try to remember different types of sums and their methods in the syllabus. This was the only solution I found to cover the syllabus in such a short time.

I pulled out the mathematics book and read. For the next three days, I was just reading and smoking. Sixteen hours a day, my eyes were on the book trying to remember each step which could save me from failing.

On the third day, I reached college for my exam. I was tense. I knew I had only read and not practiced anything. I saw Vaidehi turning the pages of her books in concentration, trying to recall formulas.

I kept looking at her, and she was giving me positive vibes, saying, I could do it again. She looked up at me blankly and continued reading her books.

This was the first time in the last one-and-a-half years that she hadn't wished me the best of luck. I passed by her and went inside the classroom. Vaidehi's seat was just next to me.

The professor distributed the question paper. The exam was tough. I tried to recall the best I could. When I turned my eyes towards her, I saw her busy solving problems.

I tried to relax and attempted those questions which I found easy. But in next one hour, I was sitting blank after completing all questions I could attempt. I don't know if I would pass or not, but I had given it my best shot.

After sometimes, I turned to see Vaidehi. She looked at me for a minute and then dropped her answer sheet on my side and kept staring at me. Without a single word or gesture, she made me understand that it was for me to copy.

I saw her answer sheet, lying near my feet. I looked at it and then into her eyes. I could have picked it up, but I was concentrating on her eyes. She knew her answer sheet had fallen and lay near me, but instead of picking it up, she kept looking at me.

She had stopped talking, and because of her I am struggling today. Why should I take her help. If she wants to help me, she must also speak to me. I am not at her mercy. I have my self-respect, and I will not take her help.

I decided that I would not take her help. I moved my eyes from her and started writing again, ignoring her sheet. And then, I moved my hand downwards and slipped her sheet back to her, looking into her eyes. The invigilator was unaware of what was going on. She kept looking at me and then took her answer sheet back. I gave her an egoistic look before carrying on with my paper.

For next the one month, I was busy in my studies and followed the same practice to complete my syllabus. And when the results were declared, only six students could pass in all five subjects, and I was one of them.

"Successful and unsuccessful people do not differ in their abilities. They vary in their desire to reach their potential." I craved her attention, and that had motivated me to clear all my exams.

My next target was to top the college in the next semester. But my eyes still missed her, my ears still missed her mesmerizing voice.

Present day
Dehradun

I logged into my Yahoo mailbox and scrolled to look for Vineet's email. I noted his number down.

After college, Vineet had joined Tata Consultancy Services and was settled in Pune. He was getting married the next week. He was in love with his colleague and wanted to settle down as soon as possible.

I dialled his number, and after a few rings, someone picked up. I could hear the sound of music, laughter and voices of people. Soon, he came to the phone. "Hello, who is this?"

"Motu! My darling, it is Rohan."

"Oh, Rohan, where are you, buddy? I sent you so many emails and even tried your number. But most of the time, you were not available," he said in excitement

Most of the time I was on site where there was no mobile network. But I was not in a mood to answer his question on mobile network.

"She wants to talk to me," I said with a smile on my face

The sound of music was loud and he could not hear me clearly and asked me to repeat myself shouting.

"I said she wants to talk to me."

"Who?" he asked.

I paused, and he replied shouting, "Are you talking about Vaidehi?"

I smiled. "Yes Motu. She messaged me. She wants to talk."

"Great news man. You made it. So speak to her," he was excited.

"I tried, but her number is switched off."

"Don't worry, try tomorrow morning again. I always knew she loves you," he replied.

"How is your wedding preparation going on?" I questioned him.

"Can't you hear the noise? All the relatives are here. Am missing you. When are you reaching?" he asked me.

I confirmed I would reach after six days. I said goodbye and went to bed waiting for the morning to hear the voice of my love Vaidehi.

The next morning, the first thing I did was dialling her number, but was disappointed as her number was still switched off. I went outside the hotel and purchased a new handset and then proceeded to the local distributor shop, which Kamal had informed me about and got a new SIM.

I asked my driver to return to Meerut, and while we were on our way, I kept on trying her number. But in vain. Why was her number switched off? I only knew, after finishing our college, that she had stayed back in Jabalpur and now taught in the same college as an ad hoc. It was surprising as she had stood second in the university, and had offers from most prestigious companies.

I tried her number a hundred times till I reached Meerut. I was worried and didn't know where she was. Then I got an idea. We could always find out the last location of the subscriber, before the phone was switched off. This feature was used to track criminals. I could always use it to find out where she was last.

I reached office in Meerut and checked the series of her mobile number. It was an Airtel number. I asked Kamal if he could check which state of India the number belonged to. As a good friend, he checked it for me and confirmed that the mobile number belonged to Madhya Pradesh.

Now the next target was to find out which location she had switched off her mobile in. I again asked Kamal to help me. He called one of his friends in the Airtel office in Indore and gave him her number. Within a few minutes, I got the information. She had switched off her mobile in Jabalpur near Shaheed Smarak Chowk.

This meant that she was still in Jabalpur. I could not miss the chance to meet her. Without wasting time, I called my boss and asked him for urgent leave for one week. He was reluctant, but then agreed.

The next day, I boarded the Mahakaushal Express to Jabalpur from Delhi. I closed my eyes and thought,

Don't walk behind me; I may not lead. Don't walk in front of me; I may not follow. Just walk beside me and be my friend.

I had studied hard in my college to beat her, but in my heart, I wanted to be with her. It was my aggression and anger which I had vented on my studies. It would not be wrong to say she was the real reason behind my success today. I sat back and relaxed and recalled the incident which took place after our fourth semester.

▼

After our third semester was over, my only aim in life was to study well to beat her in the fourth semester exams. I didn't go home in the third-semester break and studied throughout, all alone in the hostel. My life had changed. I studied for twelve hours a day. I had many friends now, and I ignored Vaidehi. She changed my life, and this was the biggest reason which proved how much I loved her.

I still remember that Sunday. Anurag came running into the hostel, shouting my name. As he opened the door of my room I said, "What happened Anurag? Why are you shouting?"

He gasped and replied "Rohan, you topped the fourth semester. You have come first! " He hugged me.

I smiled and was numb in shock. I sat down on my bed. I could feel the tears in my eyes, but I didn't allow them to flow.

"What about her, did you check her result?" I asked Anurag.

He sat next to me with his hands on my shoulders and replied, "She's come second."

I didn't know whether to be sad or happy, but I was sure now she would answer all my questions.

I reached college and looked for her, along with Anurag and Vineet. Someone informed me she was sitting in the sun on the terrace of the college building. Without wasting time, I rushed towards her and found her sitting with Reena.

I walked up to her; she was looking fairer that day. Her eyes were swollen; maybe she had cried because she hadn't topped. I reached her and stopped in front of her while she kept ignoring me. Since she left me, her skin was glowing, getting fairer by the day. I wanted to kiss on her ever so fair cheeks again.

"Can we talk?" I questioned her standing in front of her. I paused for some time and then questioned her again, but she didn't reply. I kept standing in front of her, waiting for her response in vain. Vineet and Anurag were also standing along with me, waiting for her reply.

"She is not interested in talking to you. Why don't you leave?" Reena interrupted, but I ignored her and spoke to Vaidehi.

"This building has three stories, and if you do not talk to me, I swear I will jump from here."

I knew she loved me and she would not let me jump.

She kept looking at her books and I knew she was not reading anything. I emphasized again, "I am not joking Vaidehi, I will jump for sure."

Hearing me, even Vineet, Anurag and Reena got scared. Reena tried to ask her by touching her hand. But she ignored her as well.

I walked to the edge of the terrace.

"Vaidehi, stop him, he has gone mad!" Anurag asked her shouting, but she sat still like a statue.

"Okay if he jumps, I will jump along with him. So please talk," Vineet told Vaidehi.

I looked at him in surprise.

Reena looked at him unblinking and then said, "Vineet, why will *you* jump?"

Anurag interrupted before Vineet could speak, "Not only he, I will also jump along with him. He is our best friend. We will live together and die together!"

What a filmy dialogue! I could not understand what was happening, I was standing on the edge of the terrace to gain the sympathy of my love and was expecting my two fool friends to stop me, but they were ready to jump along with me.

"Vaidehi, I will count till three, and if you don't talk, I will jump," I informed her, while she stood up, looked into my eyes and went towards the stairs.

"Yes Vaidehi, we will also jump along with our friend," Anurag added but she went on without looking at us.

I was sure, my friends were just trying to pressurize her, but I was not joking. I counted. With every count, her steps slowed down and I expected her to speak. But as I hit three, I jumped saying "Bye Vaidehi!" While falling I saw Anurag and Vineet, flying next to me, falling. Shit! They had both jumped with me.

Reena ran towards us to check, while we were moving towards the ground. I still don't believe that Anurag and Vineet had jumped with me. Soon there was the sound of three bodies crashing into the grass.

Everyone ran towards us. I saw Anurag lying to my left and Vineet to my right with both his hands upwards. I stood up immediately. Don't know how, but I was unhurt except for a few bruises. The two however were not so lucky and were rushed to the hospital. Vineet broke both his hands and Anurag broke his leg.

After that incident, I realized that I had lost Vaidehi forever because even an incident, in which I could have died, had not broken her muteness. She did not love me anymore. I was sure then and decided to move on with my life with her memories.

Every semester I studied harder and tried to compete with her. Her muteness transformed me. Rohan Verma, a second division student in his school, was topping in the engineering college. I, who had been the most shy in my school, was the most active and friendly person in college. I went the gym to keep myself fit.

I had a lot of friends now and too little time to spend with them. With every passing day, I was succeeding in my life, smiling, while she looked more tense, worried, annoyed and surprisingly fair.

I don't know how, but her muteness brought positive changes in my life. But in my heart, I always missed her voice of love.

Present day

The next day, I reached Jabalpur. After freshening up in the restroom of the railway station, I redialled her number, but it was still switched off.

I had tried to forget her in the last five years; I tried to erase her from my memories, but she came back again with a wave of hope. I must not enter the same mode of negativity but end this in one shot. Either she must come along with me hand in hand or must leave my memories forever.

I decided to go straight to her house and meet her face to face. I walked towards her house, carrying a bouquet of red roses. The lane was silent, with one or two people passing by. It was nostalgic, coming back to the most beautiful place in the world – where I learned how to love.

I opened the main gate and walked to the main door which was closed. I pressed the doorbell and kept waiting for someone to open the door. While standing, I looked around and found her garden in a bad state. The plants had not been watered and were withering. I rang the bell again, but no one answered.

Hearing me, her neighbor came out.

"Hello, do you want to meet Mr Sharma?" he asked me from the other side of the boundary wall. I nodded to confirm, and he continued. "His daughter is not well and has been admitted in the National Hospital near Shaheed Smarak Chowk."

I was shocked to hear this. Vaidehi was not well and was in hospital. Now I could understand why her mobile had been switched off and why the last location of her mobile was Shaheed Smarak Chowk. "What happened to her?" I asked him.

"She has not been well for many years; they are worried about her."

I thanked him for the information, and with a disturbed mind, I ran outside and asked the driver to drive me to Shaheed Smarak Chowk.

I reached National Hospital in twenty minutes. "Vaidehi Sharma, can you please tell me her room number?" I asked the receptionist. She checked on her computer and then replied "Vaidehi Sharma, second floor, bed number twelve, ICU."

What? She was in the ICU. What had happened to her?

I rushed towards the stairs and ran up to the second floor in a hurry. As I reached outside ICU, I asked the nurse sitting there, if I could see Vaidehi Sharma. Hearing me, an old man sitting on the chair outside the ICU stood up and tapped my shoulder. "Rohan, come along with me."

I looked surprised that he knew my name, as I had never seen him before in my life.

I followed him. He went back to the same seat where he was sitting and asked me to sit next to him.

"She had always told me, 'Papa, Rohan will come for me one day. Worried for me but I hope he comes before I die'."

He spoke with tears in his eyes. He was Vaidehi' s father. But why he was saying that? What had happened to her? Was she fine?

He continued, "Aplastic anemia is a rare disease in which the bone marrow and the hematopoietic stem cells present there get damaged. This causes a deficiency of all three blood cell types – red blood cells, white blood cells, and platelets. Aplastic refers to the inability of the stem cells to generate mature blood cells. It is most prevalent in people in their teens and twenties."

I had never heard about this disease before and listened to him. "She was detected with this illness about five years back. She is the most loveable daughter a father can have. She is not only my daughter, but my best friend. She shared every small thing with me. I knew she loved you and I knew how much pain she was in. With every passing day, her body was getting anemic. She was going pale and white, but she remembered you every day of her life. Two days back, she asked me to message you. She wanted to talk to you, but you never called her back. In the night, she had shortness of breath and irregular heartbeat and was shifted to the ICU." He pulled out his glasses and wiped his tears.

I kept looking at him. Then I got down from the seat and sat at his feet. Holding his legs I asked, "Uncle, your tears are saying a lot. But please tell me, will she be okay?"

He heard me and then cried, almost yelling in pain. I understood she was seriously ill. Tears poured out of my eyes. I needed someone to hug me. I stood up and asked the nurse, "May I meet Vaidehi?" She looked at me and then towards Uncle, who was also crying, and he gestured to her to allow me. She asked me to follow her. It was a big room with three beds and Vaidehi was lying in the one at the centre. The other two were empty.

My feet were heavy and I dragged myself to her. The constant beeping of the ventilator was hammering in my head. The nurse pulled the curtain aside and I saw Vaidehi, lying on the big bed of the ICU. Many wires were attached to her. Her face was covered with an oxygen mask. Her eyes were closed and her breathing was heavy. My most beautiful gift was lying in front of me, losing her life. I moved to her side, unblinking and sat on the seat next to her. The nurse walked out after checking the drips. I kept looking at her, and it seemed she would stand up and say "Rohan, now I can talk to you because I love you."

I spoke softly to her, "Vaidehi, I love you..." I paused, then continued. "You know when you stopped talking, everything in my life stopped. I was shattered. You were the only love I had in my life, and your voice was my medicine. Since you ignored me, I ignored my life, but every day I wanted to live, as I believed one day you would come running, hugging, kissing to me.

"Now stop playing this game of muteness and get up, my love. You have been mute since the last five years, but now you must speak."

But she was silent. "Get up Vaidehi, enough of your attitude."

I looked at her and stood to move in front of her. I touched my hands with her legs and went close to her. "Hey Vaidehi; you touched me with your feet, give me your hand, I need to say sorry. Hey come on, lift your hands and pass them to me. Vaidehi, listen, get up baby..."

I pulled her hand towards my face, kissed it and touched it to my forehead and waited for her to open her eyes. But as I left her hand, it fell back on the bed lifeless.

I cried at her, "I love you... please help me. Sit with me; hold my hand. Talk to me. Call me your friend. Look into my eyes because I'm falling."

I waited, wide-eyed, heart in my mouth, hoping for a reply. I needed to be soothed like a child.

And then there were hot tears, falling fast and thick onto my sweater.

"You know, sweet angel, I've always appreciated your spark and zest, you're a go-getter, a survivor. I like that; you are going to be just fine."

I wiped my tears and kissed her on her forehead and went outside.

"Uncle, where can I meet the doctor under whose observation she is?" I asked.

He told me it was Dr Chawla and his cabin was on the ground floor. I took the stairs and went to meet him. He was a middle-aged doctor and looked experienced.

"Sir, I wanted to know about Vaidehi."

"And, who are you, my son?" he asked me.

I paused and then replied, "Sir, I am her fiancé, Rohan." I knew I was telling a lie, but my inner feelings pushed me into saying that.

"Rohan, I can understand your concern, but as you told me you are her fiancé, I will not lie to you. We are trying our level best, but she is in a very critical condition now," he explained to me about Aplastic anemia, and he informed me that she was under treatment since the last five years.

I was losing her by the passing of every single second, I realized. She couldn't do this to me, not again. I was cursing god, who had muted my girlfriend five years back and now he was muting her forever. I came out of his cabin without hope.

I went back to Uncle who was waiting with Vaidehi's mother. I went to them and touched her feet. She looked at me with surprise and then asked me to sit. I took a seat next to her.

My love was resting inside, all alone, in the silence of her own.

"Hope you will be our son-in-law, someday," she spoke tenderly and wept.

I placed my hands on her shoulders and hugged her. "We stopped speaking to each other, maybe we could not marry, but in the heart of hearts, we both knew how much we loved each other. When I was alone, I used to talk to her in my mind, like she was with me. I will always be your son."

She burst into tears, "She cried many times for you, she always told me how much she loved you. I asked her many times to stop ignoring you and tell you the truth, but she was adamant."

My tears were flowing down and my voice trembled. "Don't worry, Aunty, my heart says she will be fine, she will get up for sure."

She continued crying like a baby in my arms.

Vaidehi's father could not control his tears. When he cried, there was a rawness to it, like the pain was still an open wound. He would clasp onto something for support, anything, a table or the back of a chair, and then his whole body would shake.

I went to him and tried to console him. "Uncle, your daughter is a fighter. She knew she was suffering from a life-threatening disease, but she let no one know about it. She kept on studying hard, to keep you happy. She knew how important her education was for you. You need to be strong for her. I am sure she will fight her way out of this."

He looked at me, "She never studied for me; I always asked her to enjoy life. I knew this day would come. But she always told me, 'Papa, I am studying for Rohan. He is studying to beat me in studies. I need to be his competitor. If I give up, he will give up.' She wanted you to succeed in your life. She was not giving you competition; she was preparing you for bigger hurdles in your life."

His words broke me down.

In college, I had studied hard to beat her. While I was thinking I was breaking her ego, unknowingly, she was supporting my ego. I always thought, she would be hurt seeing me scoring a higher rank. Unknowingly, she was the happiest person to see me score more than her. How bad was my soul and such an angel she was!

I cried as if my brain was being shredded from the inside. From my mouth came a cry so raw that even the eyes of the strangers around filled with tears. I grabbed onto a chair so that my violent shaking would not cause me to fall, and from my eyes came a thicker flow of tears. The whole world had vanished for me; now there was only pain. Pain that was enough to break me, pain sufficient to change me beyond recognition.

I gathered myself, moved to the side and dialled my home number to talk to my parents. Papa picked up the phone. "Hello?"

"Papa, it's me, Rohan."

"How are you Rohan? Calling during your office hours?" he asked.

My voice shivered while I spoke to him "I am not in Meerut. I reached Jabalpur in the morning."

"Jabalpur? Some official work?"

I tried speaking, but my voice trembled. Tears filled my throat. "No... Vaidehi..."

He understood I was crying, "What? What happened to Vaidehi? She was your batch-mate, I remember."

"Papa... she is leaving me... I need your hug." And I burst into tears.

"Where are you? Tell me, I am coming immediately," he said in tension.

I told him the hospital address, as well as about her condition and kept phone down hearing his last words, "Rohan, your mom told me long back that you loved her. I was not aware of how serious you were about her, but from your voice, it's clear how much you love her. Don't be broken, give your best to her. Maybe her eyes are closed, but her soul will be listening to you. Be with her. I am coming soon."

I went back to the ICU and sat next to her. I wiped my tears and kept looking at her. I had observed her growing fairer in the last five years, but never knew she was losing herself to a disease. "How can you be so selfish Vaidehi? You could have told me. We could have made the most of every moment."

I was sitting next to her when her father came inside and pulled out an envelope from his pocket and kept in on my lap. I looked at it with tears in my eyes. "She knew you would come one day, and she asked me to hand this over to you," he said.

I took that envelope and stood up. Tears were streaming down my eyes endlessly. I wanted to go and hide somewhere. It was six in the evening. I went outside the hospital and walked along the busy roads of Jabalpur, holding her envelope in my hand.

I called an auto and asked him to take me to RK College of Engineering. I tried to stop my tears, but every time I did so, her memories brought them out again. In the next twenty minutes, I was at the main gate of my college.

The college campus was empty in the evening; the street lights were on. I entered the gate and walked slowly, remembering the beautiful moments spent with her there. My eyes drifted to the classroom where I had seen her first, dancing on the desk. I could still feel her presence. I went to the corner behind the trees, behind the classrooms. This was a corner where we used to hide while we bunked class. The corner where she had first kissed me.

I stood in the corner, and looked at the same old walls. Tears rolled down my cheeks as I opened her envelope with trembling hands.

I opened the envelope and pulled out the letters inside and began to read them.

"*My dear Rohan,*

I will start with the words you must be missing me for a long time. I stopped talking to you and I ignored you, but one thing which I never stopped is loving you.

You might hate me by now, you might forget me by now, you might have found someone better than me, but you can never find someone who can love you more than me.

As I started reading, strange feelings rumbled inside me. Tears burst forth like water from a dam, spilling down my face. My chin trembled as if I were a small child. I breathed heavier than I had ever before. I was gasping for air that wasn't there. My throat burned forming a silent scream as I read further.

By the time you read this letter, I will be looking down on you from heaven. But you need to promise me; you will not let your tears flow. I made a mistake of making you fall in love with me, but tried to correct my mistake as I came to know I could not be the best option for you for your entire life.

After our second semester break, Papa once came to your hostel, when I informed him about us and how much I loved you but he left broken, listening to everyone in your hostel shouting my name to call you. When he informed me about this, I was very angry with you, and I decided to stop talking to you, as you had not kept your promise to keep our relationship a secret. I was angry with you, but had not expected to stop talking to you forever. I scolded you when you called me that night from Sagar. But that was the hint god gave me – to handle you and our love. Few days after that, I came to know I was suffering from Aplastic anemia and my life was short.

I was in pain. I wanted to come and hug you, wanted to be with you during my last days, but how could I be so selfish.

I decided to ignore you; I wanted you to go back to Navya. I wanted you to forget me and find someone better than me.

When you got hurt and broken, I was the one who cried every night. When you informed me you would not budge from outside college till I talk to you, I was tense and worried. I informed Akash to check on you, leaving a message for him at your hostel STD booth, without disclosing my name. I came that night, outside the college to check, but felt happy to find you had left.

When you were sick and in trouble, I tried my best to help you out in all ways I possibly could. When you smoked and took puffs to get my attention, it burned me deep in my heart.

I studied hard, to make you study harder than me. It was my dream to see you become most successful.

You always felt Vineet, Akash, Anurag, Reena and Chaaru were on your side in our love game, but you never knew they were doing what I wanted them to do. I wanted them to be on your side; I wanted them to support you, I wanted them to be your friends.

When you jumped from the terrace, you thought I never came to look for you, but you never knew that there were two ambulances which left the college that day, as I had collapsed hearing you had jumped.

You would think why I am telling you all this now. Do I want to be great?

No, Rohan. I never wanted to be great. I am writing all this because I never want you to describe me to your kids as an egoistic, selfish, arrogant girl, whom you once loved.

I am writing this to tell you how much I loved you. Please forgive me for all the pain I have given you, please forgive me for hurting you, please forgive me for loving you, please forgive me for making you love me, please forgive me for leaving you, please forgive me for being mute.

I love you with my aura, placing it about you like the deepest star-filled sky. Space and time have no meaning for my love, for it is boundless, eternal. It is a love that self-sustains through the meanest of winters, its own heat and light being the warmth, the hope. Even if you were cold to the core, my love, I would wake you like the spring wakes a flower and watch you grow, watch you bloom. Everything I am is yours... all I ask is that you take care of yourself in the same way you would care for a person you love completely; in the same way I love you.

Never have any regrets in your life, never have any regrets about me. I was happy to be loved by you. I was glad to be in your dreams. I was the luckiest girl to kiss you.

Promise me you will not smoke anymore. Promise me you will marry a girl better than me. Promise me you will fulfill your dreams. Promise me you will smile forever. Promise me you will forget me.

You got hurt because I stopped talking to you, but my muteness had many words hidden in them. Hope one day you will be able to translate my muteness and understand the feelings of your mute girlfriend.

Every day, I spoke several words in my mind. While I was mute, I was in conversation with you, and when I would die, I will still be in conversation with you. You will hear my voice in the sound of the wind, you will hear my voice in the sound of rain, you would hear my voice in your smile. I will be speaking to you forever; you just need to feel me.

Whenever it would rain, I would be saying I love you. Whenever someone smiles, I will be saying I love you. Whenever you breathe, I will be saying I love you.

I will love you from the skies; I will love you from the stars. May you forget me someday; this is what I pray.

Love you, forever.

Your mute girlfriend,
Vaidehi

Tears flowed like a river from my eyes; I was broken. Holding her letter to my face, I was crying aloud. I shouted her name, in the fear of losing her. She had made me what I was today, but had taken everything from me which I had because of her.

I was sobbing when I heard the sound of a scooty coming inside the campus. I stood up and peeped behind the wall, to check.

It was her, riding on her scooty, coming straight towards me. Wearing a white salwar suit, a glow on her face, smiling. Her hair was open. I could sense her smell from a distance. She parked her scooty and came towards me; I kept watching her. My tears were dry now. Unblinking, I was watching her enigma. She was blushing with a glow on her face. I couldn't move my eyes from her. I went up to her.

She came and held my hand and dragged me to the corner behind the trees without speaking anything, but her smile was saying a lot. She pulled me leading to an outstay on the wall. She came closer, and I could feel her breath again.

"You said my love wasn't like a new song, but like opening a book and finding a language, you'd never seen before? I want you to know I feel the same way. Your love is something beautiful; meeting you is like meeting an enigma. I don't understand how you exist in this world, yet you do. So, let me tell you now, I will always love you in mind, body, and soul. You are the trap I've wanted to fall into my whole life. I am the softness you seek, and you are the cradle for my head and heart."

She paused while I kept looking at her and continued, "I will love you forever."

Her lips were glossy, asking me to kiss her again.

Her kurti was touching my shirt, and I was feeling shy.

My heart stopped beating, my eyes closed and then I felt her glossy pink lips over my lips. Yes, she was kissing me again. Her lips tasted great and then, she pulled my hand and placed it on her waist, still holding my other hand. Looking deep into my eyes, smiling, as we took steps to dance in the silence of love. Her eyes were singing; the heart was giving music as we moved below the trees, holding each other's hand. She placed her head on my chest, and we kept moving our feet in the dance of love when I heard my mobile vibrating.

I opened my eyes and found I was standing all alone in the darkness. She was not there; It was an illusion of her. I pulled out my mobile. It was her father calling me. I picked up the phone and heard something which muted my whole life, "Vaidehi has left us all alone."

The mobile dropped from my hand. My heart stopped beating. I felt there was no land beneath me and I cried out loud.

I ran towards the main gate, letting my tears fall. I found no rickshaws, so started running on the road. I was running fast, losing my breath, shouting her name as if she was moving ahead, leaving me behind all alone. I could feel her moving on her scooty, and I was running behind her. Then I slipped and tumbled on the road. I kept sitting there, crying loudly till I found a taxi to take me to the hospital.

I rushed back to the hospital and saw her body wrapped in a piece of cloth. Her life-supporting equipment had been removed. Her father was sobbing, holding her mother in the corner. Her brother was completing the formalities to take her body, with tears in his eyes.

As I walked to her, my legs went heavy; my heart was crying, my head was bearing the burden of sins. My hands were shivering when I tried to remove the cloth from her face.

There, she lay in peace and calm. Like she was free from all burdens. Her face was still smiling; her lips still glossy.

One last time, I touched her feet and moved to her side, close to her ears and spoke softly, "Vaidehi, by mistake you touched me with your feet, would you mind offering me your hand, so I can touch and say sorry." I paused, wiped my tears and continued.

"Please Vaidehi, you can't let me do this sin, please forward your palm and let me touch… one last time…."

But she remained silent. This time, she didn't forward her hand smiling at me, this time she didn't gesture at me, this time she didn't show any attitude.

I kept glancing at her, with my eyes brimming with tears. God cannot be so wicked. I held her hand and picked up her head to hug her. She was not clinging to me anymore. Her body was cold; her eyes were closed. I wished to hug her close; I wished to embrace her once more, but she had left me all alone in this world of muteness.

Everything which I had expressed to her in real life or in dreams was true. I loved her, and I would keep loving her was the truth of my life. I cried bringing her close to my chest. My tears were making her face wet. I was crying, sobbing, and hugging her when my eyes went to her handkerchief below her pillow. I pulled it out and gently wiped her face which had become wet from my tears.

Her father came from behind, with a heavy heart and pulled me and hugged me. I cried like a baby.

"We will take her for the last rituals tomorrow morning,"

he informed me. The ambulance arrived, and her body was wrapped and taken by the hospital staff. We followed her in tears, not wanting to leave her for a second. Her mother was crying loud; her brother was holding her for support.

My mobile rang, it was Papa calling me. As I picked up and broke down without saying a word. "Where are you, Rohan? I have reached Jabalpur. Stop crying beta," he consoled me.

I told him to come to her house as we were leaving with her body. I messaged him the address.

As her body was taken to her home, I followed the ambulance sitting in an auto, crying and remembering her in my memories. As my auto moved in front of my college gate, I asked him to stop for some time and wait till I return. I wanted to feel her presence in a place where I met and fell in love.

With a heavy heart, I walked to the class where I had met her the first time. As I entered the class, my eyes went still on the bench where she had stood dancing, moving her head and hands, making me fall in love.

I sat on the chair where she uses to sit next to me and moved my legs to feel her presence again, but could only find emptiness.

She would be no longer sitting beside me; she would no longer smile at me, she would no longer gesture to me. Thoughts were overtaking my mind and soul. I was missing her deeply.

I kept crying and left the campus, never to return, boarded the auto and went to her place.

As I reached her house, I saw a mob of people and her relatives gathered outside. I crossed them and saw her body placed on the floor and many eyes filled with tears. She was smiling like her picture placed above her head.

My mind still could not believe she had left me all alone. I moved to her and sat next to her and spoke to her, "Vaidehi, enough of your attitude. See, everyone is so tense; your father is crying, your mother is crying. But I know you are just trying to be mute and ignoring us. Stop this game of muteness and get up to speak now. You can't make us cry like this. I survived when you stopped talking, but don't do this with your parents. They love you more than me."

I was talking to the still and cold body as the others with moist eyes were looking at me. My papa came and tried to pull me up. I looked at him with pained eyes. "Papa, she is Vaidehi. I always wanted you to meet her. She has not been talking to me since a long time, but I know she loves me."

I turned to her and spoke. "Vaidehi, see Papa has come to meet you. You asked me earlier if you must touch his feet or not. He is here to hug you today. Please get up. Let's take his blessings for our future."

Papa pulled me up and hugged me with tears in his eyes. "Papa please ask her to get up, she is not listening to me. She has been ignoring me for the last five years."

I spoke to her father. "Uncle, you tell her to talk to me. She is not talking to me. She loves you a lot, she will surely listen to you."

My father came once more to me and hugged me. I shouted while Papa kept holding me "Vaidehi... Vaidehi... stop this now, get up and call me stupid...please..."

I kept shouting and crying till I fainted.

It was two in the morning. I was sitting down in the corner looking at her unblinking. Her father was standing outside in the garden, discussing something with one of his relatives. My Papa had gone away to our relative's place for the night, but I stayed over there with her.

I was abusing myself for not realizing her love for me. She had loved me, and her letter was proof in my hand. I stood up and moved straight to her father.

"Uncle, may I request something to you?"

He placed his hand on my shoulder and nodded. I passed on to him the letter which she had written to me. He opened it and read it with tears in his eyes.

"Hope you can figure out how much she liked me. I want to request something, please don't say no," I begged him.

"Please let me know beta, what can I do?" he asked me

"May I marry her before her body leaves us?"

He seemed astonished and questioned me with a trembling voice. "What are you saying, Rohan? She is dead beta, and the dead do not marry," he cried.

"Uncle, please understand, we are humans and we know her body is dead, but her soul is alive and she will watch us from somewhere. Please don't say no to me. I want her to be happy wherever she is."

I pleaded with him with tears in my eyes. He kept looking at me and then went inside to talk to her mother. I waited outside for his decision.

He came out in some time while I kept looking at her. His eyes spoke his answer. He kept his hand on my shoulder and hugged me while her mother looked at me with tears in her eyes standing at the door.

The next morning, everyone gathered for the rituals. Papa also came and got to know about my decision. I was sure he would object to my decision. He came close to me and took me aside. "Are you sure Rohan?" he asked me looking into my eyes.

"Papa, would you like to see an incomplete Rohan throughout your life?" I asked him.

He kept looking at me for sometimes and then hugged me. "I am proud of you my son. Today I am proud to be your father."

His words energized me.

I went inside and saw Vaidehi's body dressed in a red lehenga, with a red scarf on her head. Her face looked white and pale, but my bride was looking gorgeous.

I knew when it started it would break me. Breaking was hard, recovery almost impossible, but of my journey, I was making the best map I possibly could. As I stood near her calm body, her mother brought vermilion in a plate. Her eyes asked me to think about my decision, but I was confident about what I was doing. Papa came behind, kept his hand on my shoulder and gestured me to complete my duty. With tears in my eyes, I picked up the red powder in my fingers and filled it in the parting of her hair.

I kept looking at her while her mother cried loudly. Papa held my shoulder from behind, and her father wiped his tears.

"Happy marriage, my dear mute wife," I broke down and dropped to my knees, crying loudly. My dad kept holding me. Soon Vineet and Anurag reached. "She has left me mute for my entire life."

Vineet hugged me as I cried loudly.

Soon, the rituals started. She was laid on the deathbed, which was carried by me from the front. Her mother and cousins yelled and cried loudly as she left the house. When I used to come to drop her during college, I never expected this day would come. As I carried her body on my shoulder, I remembered how we both had carried the scarf above my sister during her wedding and how she had gestured to me about the wedding rituals. She always wanted to be married; she loved the rituals of a wedding. But instead, her last rites were being performed.

As we reached the cremation ground, my legs went heavy; my heart stopped. Fear was taking over my mind. I was losing her forever. After sometime I would only see her only in pictures. I wanted to hug her tight and not leave her, but the time had come to say goodbye.

Her face looked smiling as though she was happy marrying me, lying on the deathbed of sandalwood. My hand touched her feet again while I was settling her still body. I picked up her hand one last time, brought it to my forehead and kissed on her cheek to say goodbye. "I am sorry, my love."

I kept looking at her closed eyes, to capture her forever in my memories. We met with a smile to end up with a silence forever.

"You need to perform her rituals as you are her husband now," her father told me.

I had chosen the toughest job of my life. Leaving my wife of a few hours to the flames.

"Please don't let me do this. I can't...." I cried in his arms.

He cried too, holding me. "No father wants to see this day. I must have committed sins in my past to see this day."

I kept sobbing and took the fire in my hand, and as I circled her body placed on the sandalwood bed. I recalled her smiles, I recalled her attitude, I recalled her dance moves, I recalled her kisses, I recalled the night when we observed the night sky, and I recalled us dancing and laughing aloud. I could only remember the best times I had spent with her, now totally forgetting her muteness.

But she still kept silent. She was my mute girlfriend and this is her story. I will always love you, till the last breath of my life, my mute girlfriend Vaidehi.

"Voice is a gift which we have received. It explains a lot when exact words are used and explained better when spoken from the heart. While I was mute, my eyes, my heart, my soul, my body, everything spoke to you Rohan. I was communicating by every means of my body. Hope I will have years to live with you, to talk to you throughout my life.

Your mute girlfriend,
Vaidehi

Email from Chaaru

Hi Rohan,

I heard about Vaidehi last night. I am settled in the US, working for Infosys. I cried the whole night for her and thought I'd mail you. I was her friend since school, and I understood her more than you. But since you entered her life, she had changed. I always felt you boarded the wrong bus as she was just opposite in nature to you, but the way she changed herself for you was admirable. She told me once how much she loved you, and listening to her, I felt that my friendship was insignificant compared to your love. When she stopped talking to you, I was with her mostly when she cried. I knew she was in pain after stopped talking to you but she never told me why. I kept asking her. I had even fought with her, but she was adamant she would not tell me what had happened. The day when you stood outside college and told her you would not move, she remained standing without food and water till she was sure that you had left. I never understood the love between both of you, but I am sure no one can love her more than you and no one can love you more than her. Now she will rest in our memories, but her presence will always be felt in our lives. May god let her rest in peace and may he give strength to her beloved husband. I am proud of you Rohan.

Your friend,
Chaaru